THE AZTEC CONNECTION

A Barkow Novel

THE AZTEC CONNECTION

Archie J. Hoagland

The Aztec Connection: A Barkow Novel

Published by Wheatmark®
1760 East River Road, Suite 145, Tucson, Arizona 85718 USA
www.wheatmark.com

ISBN: 978-1-62787-342-0 (paperback)
ISBN: 978-1-62787-343-7 (ebook)
LCCN: 2015915466

PUBLICATIONS BY ARCHIE J. HOAGLAND

Poetry of Sartor
2006, D—N Publishing, 54 pages

The Collection
2010, D—N Publishing, 517 pages

The Mystery of Sorrows
2014, Wheatmark Publishing, 287 pages

The Aztec Connection
2015, Wheatmark Publishing, 224 pages

This book is dedicated to Agnes Jeanette Hoagland,
my wife, soul mate and best friend

ACKNOWLEDGMENTS

MY HEARTY THANKS to my Publisher Sam Henrie, president of Wheatmark Publishing, Grael Norton, acquisitions manager, Lori Leavitt, my project manager, and Atilla Vekrony, website guru, plus all the folks at Wheatmark Publishing for making this publication a success as well as, in my opinion, a work of art.

Special thanks to the Green Valley Writer's Forum, who critiqued this book, page by page, chapter by chapter, as it was being put on paper and never missed a chance to compliment or criticize the written word. Good friends all.

Lastly, I thank my beautiful wife, Jean, for putting up with me as I spent countless hours pounding the keys, bringing the story to life.

PROLOGUE

GEORGE BENNET BARKOW is dangerous when provoked. His past is linked with the wealthiest woman in the world, although he's well acquainted with paucity, having breathed both the corruption of wealth and the misery of poverty. Trained in covert phases of life and death by the sub-secret Delta Force, Barkow is a man to be reckoned with. Tread lightly in his presence or suffer the wrath of his discontent. He considers trustworthy friends to be extensions of himself, and therefore defends their comfort and well-being as though they are parts of his physical reality. Love and worship are not distinguished as separate entities in Barkow's mind.

CHAPTER ONE

HIS CELL PHONE vibrated as Barkow handed his ID and boarding-pass to the flight attendant, then walking down the slanted loading ramp connecting plane to airport, the phone vibrated again. He flipped open the cover and spoke into the mouthpiece, "Barkow."

"Hi Boss, Bobby here. Have you heard from Laura today?"

"Hey, Bobby, hang one." Barkow stepped through the open door-hatch and entered the plane. He located his first-class seat, stuffed his carry-on in the overhead compartment and dropped into the comfortable cushions.

"Yes, I spoke with her at lunch today," he answered. "What's up?"

"She has not come in to work yet. I called her cell a while ago but got no answer."

"That's odd. She told me she was going in early to work on the books. What time did you call?"

"Around 4:00. I have the place open. Terry and I are here with a few customers.

"Thanks for calling Bobby. I'm on a plane that's about ready to take off but I'll see if I can reach her."

"Okay, let me know if you talk to her."

Barkow ended the call and at once called Laura's cell. It rang several times before someone answered.

"Buena's notches, Barkow. We got your woman."

"Who are you?" Barkow's voice had a growl hidden just beneath the words as he rose from his seat and reached for the overhead bin and his carry-on.

"If you wanna keep her safe, you don't go to Belize, amigo."

1

Barkow, now holding the phone clamped to his ear, was already in the process of forcing his way through the incoming passengers heading for their coach seats.

"Sir," the hostess said, "You cannot leave the cabin now. Please return to your seat."

Barkow brushed past her saying, "I'm getting off, now!"

He pushed out through the planes door and began forcing his way through down-coming traffic, on the loading ramp's decline.

"Hey man," the Hispanic voice sounded in his ear.

"Why you on a plane? I'm tellin' you. We got your woman and if you go—

"Shut up and listen," Barkow growled into the phone. I'm off the damn plane. If you're holding Laura, I want to speak with her right now."

"You supposed to go Belize tomorrow, man"

"Are you deaf?" Barkow, now angry, snarled into the phone. "Either I speak to Laura right now, or we got no fucking deal."

He pushed his way up the ramp through irritated, incoming passengers to where a flight attendant was checking boarding passes from the line to board the plane. Barkow muffled his phone and muttered, "I'm terminating my flight, here's my boarding pass." He shoved the paper in her hand and strode into the terminal. As he hurried towards the exit, the Hispanic voice spoke in his ear.

"You can speak to your woman, man, when we know you no go to Belize."

"You must be a stupid pendejo." Barkow spoke in a low, menacing voice into the phone. "I care about the woman. I will not go anywhere until she is safely back with me." Barkow said, now striding through the long-term parking lot. "If you don't let me speak with her I will assume she is dead and get back on the plane for Belize."

"No amigo, don't do that. Everything is going to be okay. I will let you talk to her. Minuto."

Barkow clicked the key remote as he approached the

Mercedes. The interior lights flashed as the doors unlocked. He heard a muffled voice say, "La perra." A door banged shut—then, "Talk to your man."

"Barkow, is that you," she said.

"It's me, Laura. If you're unharmed simply say, yes."

"Yes."

"Good, listen very carefully. I will find you. Don't do anything to antagonize them. Stay as calm as possible and I will get you back safely. Now let me talk to their leader."

"Thank God, Barkow. I'll be waiting for…." She was cut off in mid-sentence and someone said.

"You are doing the right thing amigo. In a few days your woman will be returned to you."

"I will need to hear her voice once every day and no harm is to come to her." Barkow said. "Entiendes?"

"Sí señor. Do not worry. Everything is going to be alright." In silence the connection went dead.

Barkow paused beside his car a moment, his mind forming a plan of action. He opened the car door, slid onto the black, leather driver's seat and made a call to Bobby, bartender of *Barkow's Blue Note* nightclub.

"Blue Note."

"Bobby, this is Barkow. Is Laura's car in the parking lot?"

"Just a sec and I'll take a look." A few moments later Barkow heard the back door slam shut. "Nope. It isn't here" Bobby said.

"Thanks. Laura has been taken hostage by someone. You are now in charge of the club until I get back to you. Do not call Laura's cell and don't tell anyone, except Terry, about what is going down."

"What happened to Laura?"

"Everything is muddled right now. When I have more information I'll call."

"Okay, Boss. I have everything here under control. Call me as soon as you can."

"Right, will do."

Barkow, sitting in the black Mercedes, recalled everything that happened starting this morning when he was awakened by his cell phone buzzing like a bee-hive. He'd rolled over and picked up.

"Barkow," he'd said.

"Good Morning Barkow, Harry here. Not too early, am I?"

"Not at all, Harry. What's new in New York?"

"The first word, for one thing," Harry chuckled. *"For another, I'm missing an airplane."*

"First, look in all your pockets."

"Not as easy as that. This is a Lancair IV-P with a price tag of $750,000."

"That's heavy. What happened?"

"You remember Precision Thrust? It's their plane and we carry the paper on it."

"It's difficult to misplace something like that. How'd they manage to lose the Lancair?"

"Seems like they had the plane at Jamaica and somehow it just disappeared. They'd hired some hot-shot agency to hunt it down and it was traced as far as Belize. They've spent the past three months trying to pick up a new lead without any luck. Now, Great-Metro is on the hook for the insurance. We stand to lose thousands if it can't be found."

"That's very peculiar, it should be easy enough to find a Lancair IV-P, especially if it's still in that part of the world."

"Well, Barkow, you were our best agent when you worked for us and if you have the time I want you to go to Belize and have a look around. All expenses are on us and you'll get 10% of the amount we save—if the plane is found.

"Sounds like a plan, Harry. I can leave day after tomorrow."

"Thanks Barkow, I'll fax to Judy the information we have regarding the plane along with the files from the agency that spent so much time and effort searching for it. I'll also include a signed contract agreement for this deal."

"Sounds good, Harry, I'll be in touch."

Barkow let his memory bring back everything that occurred

since that morning phone call from the CEO of Great Metro Insurance and before he boarded the plane for Belize. The scenes played in his mind like a video as he remembered.

We ended the conversation and I'd put my cell phone on the nightstand. The morning was spent checking with various contacts, gathering information about Belize and settling my affairs to be away from Phoenix for an extended time. That afternoon Laura and I had sat in the corner booth of a café near her apartment.

He replayed their conversation clearly in his mind.

"How long do you plan to be gone," she'd said.

"It all depends on what I find. It could be a couple of days or possibly weeks."

"I'll miss you stopping by for a drink at night. Who will I sing to?" She'd pouted.

Her familiar gardenia-scented perfume had lent perfection to his mood.

"I will miss you also," I'd said. "I think you're becoming a habit"

"One I don't want you to break." She'd smiled.

"No chance. You're doing a great job of running the Blue Note. Is there anything we need to discuss before I leave?

"Not really," she'd answered. "If something comes up I can always call you."

"Belize has some remote areas and it's possible you may not be able to get through at times. I bought you a going-away gift."

You shouldn't have." She'd said as she tilted her head down and away. The mannerism had been done while looking at him from the corners of her eyes with half lowered lashes.

"This is a satellite phone". I'd said, handing her the device. "You can reach me anywhere in the world."

"How touching. I shall keep it with me always."

I'd smiled again. "I'll miss the afternoon lunch with you, Laura, but now I need to make a few more arrangements before I leave. I'll call you tonight from Belize."

"Take care of yourself on the trip and call me more than once. I'm going from here to the Blue Note to do some bookwork."

We'd both stood up, ending the lunch. Our routine was to often have lunch in the afternoon, before Laura went to work at the nightclub. We'd each gone to our parking space. Rolling out of the parking lot I had driven across town to the Phoenix office of Great-Metro Insurance.

Barkow let his thoughts follow his earlier actions.

"Hi Judy, how are things going in the insurance world?"

"Hey, Barkow, same old grind. I received a fax for you from the main office. It's on your old desk."

"Thanks, Judy. I'll take a look."

I'd stepped into that office, now unused since I was no longer an employee of Great-Metro. I'd worked here as senior claims adjustor for four years, before buying the Blue Note nightclub. Now, working privately, I had a deal with Harold Goodfellow, the CEO of Great-Metro, where I only took cases that required my expertise. This was the first time since I'd quit, that they'd called for my help.

At 7:30 this evening, I'd been at Gate 3, awaiting the call to board for Belize. Now, it's 7:55 and I'm back in the Mercedes, in a depressing mood and Laura's been kidnapped.

CHAPTER TWO

THE BLACK MERCEDES sped through the warm Arizona night. Barkow's thoughts continued to analyze his situation as he drove straight to Laura's apartment. Barkow took the steps to the second landing two at a time. At her apartment he located the key to her door and let himself into the residence. Everything seemed to be in order with no sign of anything out of the ordinary.

He stopped looking around and let his thoughts analyze the situation: *That little jerk on the phone seemed surprised and said I was not supposed to go to Belize until after tomorrow. For some reason they don't want me there.*

Barkow stood in the center of the great-room. In his mind a melody slowly pulsated along with his thoughts.

Those guys who have Laura, had to have taken her between the times we had lunch today and when I boarded the plane.

The reason hit his brain like a hammer blow.

There is a mole either at Great-Metro or Precision Thrust. That's the only way anyone in Arizona could possibly know I planned going to Belize the day after tomorrow.

He pulled his cell and called Detective James Greenwell of the Phoenix Police Department.

"Greenwell."

"Hi, Jim, Barkow here. You busy?"

"I'm home watching TV. What's up?

Barkow quickly filled the Detective in on the details. "So she must have been grabbed shortly after we had lunch today," he finished.

7

"Sounds that way, have you found her car?"

"No, but it's not at the Blue Note or in her parking place at her apartment. Can you put a BOLO out on it?"

"Yeah, I can and will. Are you sure they were Hispanic who called you?"

"He spoke some Spanish and sounded like he was young, maybe eighteen to twenty-four."

"I'll call the Gang-Squad leader and fill him in. He may know if something is going down."

"Good. I'll see you first thing tomorrow. When will you be at the precinct?"

"I check in at seven. You want to meet for breakfast?"

"Yes. See you around 6 a.m. at the La Cholla."

"See you then, Barkow. Don't worry, we'll get her back."

🕐 The next morning at 6:05 Barkow walked into the Mexican restaurant. He took a table by the back wall and ordered coffee. Detective James Greenwell came in a few minutes later.

"Morning, Jim," Barkow said. "Were you able to contact the Detective of the Gang-Squad?"

Greenwell pulled back a chair and sat down. "Yes, and he had a bit of information."

"What'd he have?"

"He said a group of Coyote Rojo are in town working with El Perro Callejero.

"What does that mean?"

"The Red Coyotes are a gang of young thugs in Tucson. They are similar to The Street Dogs in Phoenix, although they're two separate gangs. Both deal primarily in drugs and are involved in strong-arm protection and robbery."

"What do you mean by, 'working together'?" Barkow said.

"Six Coyotes have been keeping company with the Dogs. It's a very unusual thing but as yet we've seen no criminal activity."

"Did you get the BOLO out on Laura's car?"

"Her car was located this morning at 3:45. It was parked at Sky Harbor Airport. It's been side-swiped along the driver side. We towed it to the Police impound lot."

"I want to take a look at it."

"We can stop by the lot right after breakfast."

"Sounds good," Barkow said as their orders arrived. "Let's eat."

🕐 IN THE OFFICE of the impound lot, Police Officer Peter Barnes greeted the two men.

"Hi Loo, haven't seen you for a while." Lieutenant James Greenwell nodded in recognition.

"Hi, Pete. We want to take a look at the blue Chevy hauled in here this morning."

"Sure thing, follow me."

Over to one side of the lot, Barkow recognized Laura's midnight-blue Chevrolet. The driver's side was badly dented and scraped from taillight to headlamp. The driver-side door handle and outside rearview mirror were broken off. Both side windows were shattered but still in place.

Barkow opened the front passenger door and leaned inside, immediately struck by a faint gardenia scent that lingered within. He opened the glove compartment and found it empty. There being nothing else of interest to Barkow and the Lieutenant, the three men returned to the office.

"Here's the stuff we took out of the car." Pete said as he laid a clear plastic bag on the counter. "You can look at it through the bag but not open it. We like to keep it clear of prints. Barkow picked up the bag and looked at the contents. A black document case that had held the owner's manual, car registration and insurance cards, assorted documentation about the car's tires, jack, etcetera. One thing of interest to Barkow was a tiny gold earring. He remembered giving the earring and necklace set to Laura on her birthday.

"From the damage to the driver side of the car, it's obvious it was forced off the road when they grabbed Laura," Barkow said.

"I have a black and white unit searching possible routes between Laura's apartment complex and the Blue Note." Jim's cell buzzed. "If we can find the mirror or door handle we will know where the kidnap took place." Snapping open his phone he said, "Greenwell." He listened a moment, then said—"Yes, I know the place. I'll be there in ten minutes."

"News about Laura?"

"Yeah. They found the car parts a half mile from her apartment. See you later Pete."

As they left the office, Jim said, "We can take my car, it will be faster." They sped through the streets with siren blaring and lights flashing to arrive at the scene of the accident a few minutes later. It had taken place in a curve, on a stretch of divided roadway that skirted a high bank of rock on one side and warehousing across the median on the other.

The skid marks on the pavement indicated the exact place the car left the road. Laura had applied the brakes and had tires skidding when forced into the catch zone at the base of the rock laden bank.

"They must have grabbed her within fifteen minutes of when we parted after lunch." Barkow exclaimed.

⊙ ARRIVING AT THE now closed Blue Note bar, Barkow parked in back and went to his office. He sat at his desk with a glass of Blanton's on ice. He took a sip of the drink as he pondered his position.

Either the Red Coyotes or the Street Dogs have Laura. They do not want me to go to Belize for a few days. Why?

He tasted the bourbon.

It has something to do with the missing Lancair which means I definitely need to go to Belize.

He swirled the ice in his drink.

They said I would get Laura back in a few days. He took another taste. *That means the plane will be out of my reach in a few days.*

He drained the bourbon in a single swallow and called Lieutenant Jim Greenwell.

"Greenwell."

"Hi Jim, Barkow here. I need to talk with your Gang-Squad leader."

"His alias is "Hombre Blanco". We never use his real name. Can I have him meet you somewhere?"

"When can he meet?"

"He is available now because it is not yet noon."

"Good. Please ask him to meet me at the Blue Note. We haven't opened yet. Just tell him to knock on the door in back marked private."

"Will do, see you later."

"Thanks Jim, see you."

🕐 AT THE SOUND of rapping on the door Barkow opened it and stared. A slender young man wearing faded blue jeans and a hooded sweatshirt stood before him. He had dark dreadlocks, a thin, skimpy beard and wore sunglasses and dirty sneakers.

"Mr. Barkow?"

"Hello, just call me Barkow. Come in and have a seat."

He entered and took a chair in front of the desk. Barkow closed the door and then sat behind the desk.

"I expected an older person." He reached across the desk offering to shake hands.

"Yeah, I know, but don't let my looks fool you." He reached forward and shook the proffered hand.

"Did Greenwell fill you in on my case?"

"No. He said you would."

"You're familiar with the Street Dogs?"

"Of course," the visitor said.

"I am certain that they, the Red Coyotes in Tucson or both,

have kidnapped Laura Logan, my Manager." Barkow said and explained all that had happened when he boarded the plane. "Putting two and two together, it is reasonable that someone in Precision Thrust, the planes owner, or Great Metro who insures it, knew I was contacted to go to Belize and took steps to stop me."

"It sounds like the sort of thing they would be up for," said the undercover officer. "I'll do some checking and see if I can pick up a lead."

"What I need," Barkow said, "is where the Street Dogs hang out, their leader's name and who is his girlfriend."

"I do not advise contact," said Blanco. "They're a tough group who mainly control the drug industry in Phoenix. I'm concerned as to why the Coyotes are involved. Normally these gangs barely tolerate each other. Now it seems they're somehow working together."

"My thoughts exactly," Barkow growled. "Are you going to give me the information?"

"To contact them, my friend, would be a grave mistake. You would find yourself full of bullet holes and laying out in the desert somewhere. Better to let me smell around a little and see what's up."

"I need to be in Belize right now. There's a damn good reason why they don't want me there. I'm not going to let some gang of punks interfere with my life. Either fork over the info or I'll find it on my own.

"Trust me, Barkow. You do not want to do this. They will eat you alive and your friend too."

"Then our business is over." Barkow stared at the man before him. "You know the way out."

"Okay, okay.... I'll tell you because Greenwell asked me to give you whatever you wanted. The pack leader is Juan Valdez. His current girlfriend is Juanita Gomez and he lives above the El Toro Cantina."

"Thanks, Blanco," Barkow said. Can I buy you a drink?

"Got any tequila?"

"Follow me," Barkow said over his shoulder as he stood

and walked out of the office and through a door leading to the interior of the nightclub. They walked across the empty dance floor and over to the bar. "What's your favorite brand?"

"I'm not particular—JC is fine."

Barkow, from behind the bar, sat two shot glasses and a bottle of Jose Cuervo Especial on the bar. As he busied himself putting salt in a small bowl and slicing up a lime he looked up at Blanco, smiled and said, "So, how long you been a cop?"

"Four years," answered Blanco, "three working with gangs."

Barkow set the salt and lime on the bar and came around to take a stool next to his guest. The young looking law enforcement officer uncapped the bottle and poured two shots of tequila. He shoved one to Barkow and pulled the salt and lime between them. They each picked up a shot-glass and raised it to each other.

"Salud, amigo," Barkow said.

"Salud," Blanco answered.

They tossed down the shot and each picked up a slice of lime touched it to the salt and squeezed it in their mouths. Barkow poured the next two.

"Salud, amigo," Blanco said.

"Salud," Barkow answered.

"I have to go to work now," Blanco said as he slid out of the barstool. He handed Barkow his card with a cell number scribbled on it. "If you get in a jam with the gang, I'm available."

"Thanks, I appreciate the offer." Barkow glanced at the written number then carefully tore the card into tiny pieces.

"You don't want my help?"

"Got it memorized. I don't want it on me if things go bad." He said as he dropped the shredded card in the trash can behind the bar.

Barkow followed the cop to the door and said, "Before you go, listen up. The guy who called me sounded like he was pretty sure that holding Laura would keep me here. For all I know they may be watching this building but I did not notice anyone tailing me when I drove here. It may be best if you wait inside a few minutes while I drive away. If they are as organized as you say they could be watching my car and keeping tabs on where I go."

"I was very watchful when I came in," Blanco said, "this place is in a residential area for the most part so I think if anyone was tailing you he would be sitting in a car where he could see yours. I saw no cars parked nearby."

"You're probably right, it was just a thought. I'll be in touch if anything comes up."

The officer left; after a few minutes Barkow got in the Mercedes and pulled out of the parking lot. He made a call to *On Star,* received the address for El Toro Cantina and headed in that direction. As he drove, his thoughts mulled over a plan working in the back of his mind.

These yahoos don't even know what I look like. They didn't know I was on the plane a day early when they called and no one is tailing me, so maybe they're not too sharp, but I'll find out.

The black Mercedes sped through the afternoon Arizona heat and a few minutes later pulled into the parking lot of the cantina. Barkow put his wallet in the glove box and took out a few plastic tie straps. He walked to the arched entrance of the brick building and went inside.

CHAPTER THREE

COMING OUT OF the bright sunshine the interior was dark and cool. Barkow stopped just inside, removed his sunglasses and took a moment to let his eyes adjust to the room. The bar ran the length of the wall opposite the entry door with a row of stools before it. There were several men playing pool on a table to his right and a few tables with chairs, all empty, to his left. He walked straight to the bar and motioned the barkeep over.

"Is Juan Valdez here?"

"Who wants to know?"

"I do."

"And you are," he said.

Barkow's gray eyes narrowed and hardened as they looked into the bartender's eyes.

"I'm the man who will make Juan very rich, unless his stupid barman does not tell him I'm here."

"Juan is still in bed. He does not come down until around four in the afternoon."

"I see." Barkow said. His cold, gray stare held the barkeep in a near magnetic grip. "I'll be back at four."

He turned away and went out the door. He glanced right and left seeing no-one as he walked around the old brick building and found an iron fire-escape attached to the back wall. Without hesitating he quickly climbed the narrow stairs. It was only a two story building and in a few seconds Barkow was peering through an open gap beneath the paint-peeling sash of a partially raised window. The room was in semi-darkness and as his eyes adjusted to the scene within, a smile broke the sternness of his features. In the bed lay two figures tangled together in the sheets. He carefully raised the old fashioned window and slipped inside. Before the pair was fully awake, Barkow had their hands cuffed together behind their backs with plastic tie-ties and was gagging them. Juan began to make a loud noise behind his gag. Barkow slapped the side of his head hard, pushing him off the bed. He knelt, putting his knee on the stomach and leaning over the terrified face, holding a finger over his lips, signing silence. The noise did not resume.

Barkow turned his attention to the naked girl. Using another plastic tie strap he attached her cuffs to the bedpost. He stepped back, pointed at her and signed the silence signal. His stare had the effect of impeding her ability to move. He tapped his chest with his right hand then held his index and middle fingers pointed at his eyes. He quickly turned his hand, slowly extended his arm and pointed both digits at the girls face. A very clear signal: I'm watching you.

"Okay, tough guy, on your feet." Barkow growled as he reached down and grabbed the naked man's hair. He jerked Juan to a sitting position, than stepped behind him. He put a hand in each armpit and stood him upon his feet. He roughly maneuvered the cuffed and gagged man over and through the window, then down the fire escape to the corner of the building, across the empty parking lot and into the trunk of the Mercedes.

The sleek black coupe sped through the afternoon sun as it left the city of Phoenix on a divided highway into the desert. The car streaked through a rocky canyon and rounded several curves before Barkow took an off ramp that later turned into a dusty, dirt road. After winding through a thicket of mesquite trees, he drove into the yard of an old, deserted line shack that was falling apart. As the car slid to a stop Barkow stepped out and popped the trunk open. He jerked the naked man from the trunk and hustled him through the dust laden air into the dilapidated building.

"What you want me for, man? I didn't do anything to you." Juan muttered as soon as the gag was taken off.

"I am a man of little patience." Barkow said as he removed an ivory handled jackknife from his pocket.

"I am going to ask you some questions. I want truthful answers. In the next ten minutes you will either be released or you will be dead."

"I'm telling you man. I don't know nothing about you." Fear made the man's eyes widen.

"Why are some coyotes hanging with your gang?"

"They just wanted some information about our turf." The trembling man blurted. "They're gonna snatch a woman. All we did was get some information on her whereabouts for them."

"Do you let anyone come on your turf and do whatever they want?"

"He paid big-time in drugs for the information. That's all I know about what went down."

"Where did they take her?"

"Back to Tucson, I guess. I swear man, that's all I know about it."

"Who runs the Coyotes in Tucson?"

"Scotty is the boss. I don't know his real name."

"Where do they hang out?"

"I don't know."

Barkow's right hand reached out and slapped the side of the bound man's head. He staggered sideways and fell to his knees. "Don't give me that shit," Barkow said as he opened the blade of the jackknife.

"They hang out at the "*Spanish Rowel Tavern*" is all I ever heard," Juan said, his eyes fixed on the knife.

"You're going to forget you ever saw me. Understand? You're never going to tell anyone about what happened to you today. Understand?"

"Okay, I understand."

Barkow reached out and slapped Juan's face again. "I just

gave you your life, stupid. Say it like you mean it or I will change my mind."

"Yes Sir. I understand and agree and thank you for my life." The terrified man said, speaking hurriedly.

Barkow put his face within an inch of Juan's nose and growled. "If you or the dogs ever bother me or mine again—I will kill you, understand?"

"Yes Sir," Juan stammered. "I understand."

Barkow put him back in the trunk, then called Blanco and made certain arrangements.

🕐 IN LATE AFTERNOON, Barkow's black Mercedes shot over the sunbaked asphalt of Interstate 10, headed for Tucson. He called "*El Toro Cantina*" on the car phone.

"El Toro," someone answered.

"I have Juan on ice," Barkow growled. "Speak to no one about his disappearance and I will not kill him."

"I understand," said the voice.

"I will return him unharmed in a day or two—*if* you follow orders, otherwise I will return only his head." Barkow cut the connection and drove on, arriving in Tucson as the sun was sinking behind the Tucson Mountains. He followed On-Star's directions and found the "*Spanish Rowel Tavern*" on the south side of the city. The building was set eighty feet back from the street with a large, unpaved parking area around it. He pulled the Mercedes between two other cars standing close to the tavern entrance.

"I need to speak with Scotty." Barkow said to the barkeep.

"People in hell need ice-water." The barkeep said as he turned to walk away.

"In that case I'll give my deal to the Dogs in Phoenix." Barkow said and headed for the exit.

"Wait up. Scotty is sitting in the booth behind the pool table." The bartender called.

Barkow changed course and went to the booth. Standing

before the man sitting down he said, "I have a deal for you, if you care to discuss it."

"Please sit down," said the olive-skinned individual in the booth. "I am always available to hear a deal."

"This one concerns a lot of money, would you prefer to talk someplace more private?"

"No. This is alright. Would you like a drink?"

"JC," Barkow said as a hint of smile cracked his lips.

The bartender brought the square bottle of tequila and two shot glasses. Scotty filled the glasses and set them in the center of the table between them.

Without touching the drink, Barkow fixed his stare upon the eyes of the man across from him and said, "Here's the deal. I have three hundred and fifty pounds of pure, uncut cocaine on this side of the border. I need a distributor to take it off my hands. It's yours for 40% of street value."

"Is it packaged?"

"No. It is in bulk form. I only offer because I am from out of state. I have no connections on the West Coast. You want in or not?"

"I need to have my lieutenant check it. Bring me a sample and…."

"Bullshit!" Barkow exclaimed. "I'm a man in a hurry. This deal goes down tonight, right now, or it won't go down at all. Get your man and come with me. He can check the stuff now, give me half of what you owe me now and send the other half in ten days to an address I'll give you."

"How much?"

"Three sixty large now and the same amount to send in ten days. You're only getting this deal because I'm in a hurry. Take it or leave it. You have ten seconds to decide." Barkow stood up and looked at the exit door as he pulled on a pair of black leather driving gloves.

"That's a little steep, considering we have to…."

Barkow turned towards the door and began walking. Two

men moved from their table and took a position blocking the exit door. As Barkow moved past the pool table he ripped a pool cue from the hand of a surprised, idle player and broke it over his knee without breaking stride. Holding the broken butt of the cue in his right hand he struck like a coiled rattlesnake at the two men by the door. The weighted end of the cue slammed against the side of the first man's head at the same time Barkow's booted foot collided with the groin of the second man. He pushed through the door between them as they both staggered and fell.

"Hey, man, I'm the real Scotty," yelled a man who had followed him through the door. "Let's talk business."

Barkow stopped and turned toward the newcomer who was wearing jeans and a muscle shirt. His skin looked pasty as if it was bleached and sunburned—he had a shock of red hair and a week old growth of beard.

"I got no time for games." Barkow said as he sized Scotty up. "You want the deal or not?"

"I got to see the stuff first."

"You and me in my car. Bring the cash and a cell phone with you." Barkow said. "I'll wait in my car for five minutes, before I drive out."

"Don't leave. I'll be right back." Scotty turned and hurried back into the tavern. Five minutes later Barkow started the car then slowly backed out and pulled towards the driveway. In the rearview mirror he saw the redhead come running after him, carrying a duffle bag. He stopped and Scotty jumped into the passenger seat.

"No tail or you're a dead man." He growled.

"No problem, man. This is too good a deal to lose. Let's go."

Barkow drove across the city and turned west on Speedway. He drove over the narrow mountain road of Gates Pass in the Tucson Mountains and down into the desert until he came to a desolate section filled with saguaro cactus and creosote bushes. He found a fairly level place where the pavement and the desert floor met, turned off the pavement and zigzagged through the plants until he was well off the deserted road, stopped and cut the lights.

"It's stashed right over there," he said, with a nod of his chin. Scotty tried to open his locked door.

"Before we check-out the bales I want to see the cash," Barkow said. His cold, gray hypnotic gaze locked on the eyes of his passenger.

"Sure thing," Scotty muttered as he pulled the draw cord on the duffle bag between his knees.

"Easy does it." Barkow spoke in a guttural voice, pointing a small automatic at Scotty. "If you happen to pull a weapon out of that bag, I'll gut-shoot you right here."

"No gun," the redhead said. "Three hundred and sixty grand, just like you asked for."

After Barkow was satisfied the count was near correct they got out of the car and walked toward the car front. The blow came from his right fist as he knocked Scotty to the ground.

"What the hell." The gang leader cursed as he rolled away and rose to a crouch while digging a clasp knife from his back pocket. Barkow waded in kicking the arm that held the knife and grabbing the opposite wrist. The knife fell from numbed fingers as Scotty was whirled around twice and sent crashing into the side of the car. Before he could form a defensive stance Barkow was raining blows upon his opponent until he folded into a fetal position covering his head with his arms.

Barkow stepped back and watched as the red haired man slowly rose to a sitting position while blood from a broken nose dripped from the tufted whiskers on his chin. Barkow squatted before the broken man, holding the clasp knife he had picked up. "You have a major problem, Scotty boy." The blade of the knife opened with an ill-omened snick.

"I didn't do you no harm," muttered the battered man. "Why you comin' down on me?"

"I should carve you up like a Christmas turkey," Barkow said as he watched the fear come into Scotty's eyes.

"Why, man? I never saw you before. What'd I ever do to you?"

"You got my girl, you little piece of shit."

"What girl? Are you talking about the blonde? Oh-h…." His voice faded. "Are you Barkow, from Phoenix?"

"You got my girl and I got you and three-sixty large."

"I got no beef with you, man. You can have the blonde. It was just a business deal."

"You and me, Scotty, are going to do a little business right now," Barkow said as he tested the edge of the knife for sharpness while his eyes bored into those of the leader of the Red Coyotes.

"Now wait a minute, Barkow." Scotty whined. "I'll give back the blonde and you can keep the cash for your trouble."

"Here's how it's going to go down." Barkow growled the words low in his throat. "You are going to call your second in command and have him bring her to the freeway underpass on Prince tonight at 3:00 o'clock. He is to come alone and if he crosses us up—you, Scotty boy, are going to die a very unpleasant death, but first, I want to know right now—who set up this little party to grab my girl?"

"It was Juan Cortes himself who called me." Scotty said quickly. "You know he's the head of the Cortes Crime Syndicate. He actually controls the drug traffic in Central America. He's got a deal going down there in Belize."

"Good. Now, Scotty boy, I want a commitment on tonight's switch."

Scotty let out a long sigh of relief as he realized he may survive the night. "I agree. Tonight at three on the dot, the Prince underpass. Come alone and you'll trade me for her."

"That's right. If he is one minute early or one minute late, the deal is off. He gets the girl and I get you. He is to enter the underpass with lights off, from the east side heading west at exactly 3:00 a.m. Pacific Standard Time and stop when I flash my lights. Laura is to be with him in the front seat. Then he is to roll down the driver's window and put both hands out so I can see he has no gun. After we make the exchange we each go our separate ways."

🕐 THE MERCEDES PURRED its way down the freeway and took the off-ramp prior to the Prince exit. It swept down the ramp and turned left where it circled through the city blocks to enter the Prince Street underpass of the freeway facing east and stopped, lights off. Exactly on time a dark sedan, with lights off, entered the underpass coming out of the east and stopped when the Mercedes flashed its lights. The two cars sat facing each other in the dark from a distance of thirty feet. Barkow approached the dark sedan from behind it. He had used his key remote to flash the Mercedes' lights. He stepped up to the car as the driver put both empty hands out the window. With a quick movement a large plastic tie-tie was looped over the extended wrists and pulled tight; Barkow almost pulled the driver through the window as he secured the cuffed wrists to the exterior rear view mirror.

"Are you okay, Laura?"

"Yes I am."

"Are you tied up or restrained in any way?"

"No."

"Good." He said as he reached through the window to her. "Take his keys from the ignition, give them to me then leave this car and go get in the Mercedes."

As she did so, Barkow opened the trunk of the rescue car and then went to the place he'd held the gang leader while they'd waited. He yanked Scotty to his feet, hands still cuffed behind him and feet tied with plastic tie-ties, leaving just enough slack to take little short steps. He hustled him to the dark sedan and stood Scotty with his back to the open trunk. Barkow brought forth an ivory handled jackknife as Scotty's eyes grew wide in fright.

"Hey, man, you said…." Barkow slapped the side of his head.

"I want you to understand that I am very serious, so listen carefully." The knife opened before the terrified eyes of Scotty, gang leader of the Coyotes. "If you ever cause me or mine any reason whatsoever to be alarmed or harmed in any way," he reached out and placed the tip of the blade against Scotty's cheek, "or if you ever hear of any harm coming our way and don't let me know," he drew the blade in a C-shaped circle, "I will personally find you and kill you." Blood ran from the cut. "Do we understand each other?"

Scotty dumbly nodded his head. Barkow pushed him backwards into the car trunk and walked back to his Mercedes. He drove the car alongside the open trunk and got out to throw in the duffle bag of money and slammed the trunk lid shut. The total exchange took place in the space of six minutes.

CHAPTER FOUR

BARKOW DROVE INTO the basement parking of his condo at 5:15 a.m. after a swift trip from Tucson to Phoenix. Laura was exhausted from the ordeal of being kidnapped and rescued in the space of a day and a half. She was asleep in the cushions of the seat with the back partially reclined.

He pulled into his regular parking space and turned off the ignition key. For a moment he gazed upon Laura's sleeping form. Her blonde hair was tousled and partly covered her face. She wore the same clothing as when they had parted after lunch two days ago. Barkow, aware she was in love with him, wondered to himself. *Could I love her without reservation? Did my love for Mary Cruthers destroy any possibility for me to love another after the way she had obliterated the unconditional love I held for her through four long years of loneliness?*

The melody from his past had reappeared in his mentality when Laura was taken and was now a constant reminder in the background. *If I can ever love anyone again,* he thought, *I know it will be Laura.* He shook his head as if to clear it and gently touched Laura on the shoulder to awaken her.

"Time to wake up," he spoke low and soft. She became aware the car no longer was moving and opened her eyes. Barkow pressed the auto button to slowly raise the seat back to an upright position. She rubbed her eyes and spoke.

"Where are we?"

"We're parked in the basement of my condo. It's time to go up."

"Go up? I need to go to my place," she murmured.

"Laura, listen to me. You were kidnapped, your car was

totaled and you were scared out of your wits. I must leave for Belize as quickly as possible. I want you to stay in my condo while I'm gone because they may try something again. Here you will be safe and I will not worry about you."

"But Barkow…"

"No buts," he said. "Right now you need to rest. You will have the satellite phone and can reach me at any time. I will have a trusted friend take you to and from work until I return. He can also take you to your apartment so you can get anything you want from there."

"Well Barkow." She said. "If you think it's really necessary."

"Of course it's necessary," he smiled. "Let's go up and I'll make the arrangements. You remember meeting Larry Fitzsimmons?"

"Yes. I remember him."

"He's a good kid and will drive you around while I'm gone. You can fill Bobby and Terry in on the details, but no one else except Jim Greenwell."

After showing Laura the guest bedroom and bath, Barkow called Larry.

"Hello," said a sleepy voice.

"Hi Larry, it's me, Barkow"

"Hey Barkow, what's up?"

After explaining what he was to do, Barkow said. "You can handle this for a couple of days, right?"

"You bet, Barkow. Anything I can do to help."

"Good. I knew I could count on you."

He gave Laura a door key, the security alarm code, Larry's phone number and told her to call him on the satellite phone whenever she wanted to talk. He assured her she would be safe in the condo. They hugged and kissed and five minutes later he was back in the Mercedes, headed for the airport once again at 6:10 a.m.

It's imperative I get to Belize before they want me to be there. Something's going down for sure and I may have already missed it, he thought, but perhaps I can still pick up a lead. Laura will be safe

enough at both the condo and the Blue Note and I have given Hank,
Jim and Larry full information on what has happened.

⊘ BARKOW ARRIVED AT Belize City International Airport with
the last rays of the evening sun. He rented a Ford Explorer from
National Car Rental and drove from the airport to the Radisson,
Fort George Hotel. The hotel was built on a peninsula and his
second floor room had an excellent view of the Caribbean and
the San Pedro Ferry's course around the peninsula. Close by was
the Baron Bliss Lighthouse, the Bliss Institute for Performing
Arts and Tourism Village.

After a quick shower and a call to Laura, he had a meal in
the hotel coffee shop and drove around the town in a crisscross
pattern to familiarize himself with the lay out of the streets. On
one particularly dark street close to the water he found what he
was looking for, *The Palms*, a local watering-hole for seamy characters. The place looked rundown and in need of a paint job. A
few cars were standing near the entrance. He parked and went
inside. The walls were dingy and the carpet well-worn in the
semi darkness. Barkow took a stool near the end of the long bar
and waited for the bartender to come over.

"What'll you have?"

"Bourbon on the rocks. Blanton's if you have it."

Without further conversation the barkeep walked back
along his back-bar and selected a bottle. He brought the
bourbon and a glass filled with ice cubes over to Barkow and
poured the glass full.

"Not Blanton's, but it's the best we have." He said.

"No problem." Barkow said and took a sip of the drink. At
the end of the room was a stage with curtains drawn. Tables and
chairs were scattered around a small dance floor. A row of booths
ran along the wall opposite the bar.

The Barkeep was washing glasses as Barkow sized up the
room. Two guys sat in a booth. Three couples sat at three differ-

ent tables and a lone woman occupied a barstool at the other end of the bar.

Barkow finished the drink, got the barkeep's attention and pointed to his empty glass. When the fresh drink arrived he placed a one hundred dollar bill on the bar and asked the barman:

"How would you like to make a few bucks?"

"Of course."

"I need to talk with someone familiar with the airplane business in Belize."

"How familiar?"

"I need a man who knows what comes and what goes, who's in and who's out."

"Nothing technical?"

"No. Nothing technical. I want a mouthpiece for the under-belly of what goes on in Belize."

The bartender reached for the bill and Barkow set his glass on it.

"You have not earned anything yet."

"One minute." The barkeep went to the lone woman at the end of the bar.

Barkow watched as the man spoke with her. Heads bobbed as they talked back and forth, sometimes glancing at him. The barkeep sauntered back.

"Rosita will speak with you."

"What would a woman know of underbellies?"

"This woman knows everything that happens in the shadows of Belize."

"We'll see." Barkow said as he picked his glass up from the bill and slid off the barstool. He walked slowly toward the woman at the end of the long bar.

She was somewhere between 35 and 45 years of age, coal black hair with a body built for pleasing a man. The two men in the booth stared at Barkow as he strolled up and sat on the stool next to her.

"Good evening, my name is Barkow. May I buy you a drink?"

"I do not want you to buy me anything. My name is Rosita."

She did not look at him but seemed to stare into the back-bar mirror. He was also keeping tabs on the two men in the booth, via the mirror, noting they still stared at him. A smile crossed his lips as he realized she was covertly checking him out.

"Is that your boyfriend in the booth?"

"That is my brother and his friend."

"I am told you have an inside track on things in Belize."

"What do you want to know?"

"Why don't you want me to buy you a drink?"

"How much is it worth to know the reason?"

He smiled and said: "The price of a drink."

"I do not allow strange men to buy my drinks."

"I'm not a stranger. I introduced myself, Rosita."

"So you did. You may buy me tequila."

Barkow snapped his fingers and the barkeep came over.

"A tequila for Rosita. Make it the best in the house and bourbon for me."

The bartender left to fix the drinks and Barkow said, "Excuse me a moment." He turned the stool around to slip off then sauntered over to the booth with the two men.

"What do you find so interesting in me, boys?"

"What do you find so interesting in Rosita?"

"She is female and easy on the eyes. You two, on the other hand, are both revolting and give me a headache. I strongly suggest you stop looking at me or I will consider it bad manners and wipe the floor up with you. By the way, you're both stupid and ugly as well."

Barkow turned and walked back to Rosita.

"Okay Rosie, it's time to get down to business. How would you like to make some money?"

"Doing what?"

"Giving me the low-down on a Lancair that was recently in Belize."

"Oh! I was hoping you wanted to go to bed with me."

"No, Rosie. I would not have to pay to bed you."

"You think you know me that well, eh?"

"Rosie, I knew I could have you when I first walked into this dump."

"Okay! So I'm a pushover for some good looking guys. So what?"

"So I want some information. You give me the right stuff and I'll make it worth your while."

"You make it worth my while Honey and I'll definitely make it worth yours."

Barkow smiled at Rosita, dropped two twenties on the bar and held out his hand in a grand gesture of showing her the way. She slipped off the stool.

"Where to?"

"Joints like this often have pick-up microphones in odd places so they can listen in on the customer's conversations. We're going to go sit in my car where I know I will not be overheard."

"Will I have to defend my virtues?"

"What virtues?"

Both laughing, they begin walking toward the exit. The two guys in the booth got up and walked in a direction to cut them off.

"Best tell your brother not to interfere or he will regret it."

Something in Barkow's speech and the look in his eyes conveyed a message to Rosita that he was absolutely certain of the outcome. She looked at the two men and shook her head. They turned around and went back to their booth.

"Good girl." Barkow said, taking her arm and leading her out the door to his car. He opened the passenger door and she climbed in. Barkow noticed a tall man in a bush hat leaning against the trunk of a tree as he went around and got in the driver's seat. He removed his wallet and counted out ten, one hundred dollar bills and laid them in a row on the dashboard.

"Tell me about the Lancair, Rosie."

"Two men in Belize were hired to deliver a plane from here to Jamaica. When they delivered the plane they needed a way to get back. They were talking to a group of bush pilots in a bar trying to bum a ride back here. A really big, black, ugly looking man tells them he has a way to help them out. He said he was in the bar looking for a pilot to fly a plane to Belize. He has no money for them, but explains it would solve both their problems. They agree and the big guy takes them to the airport and there sits a beautiful, red and white, Lancair IV-P. They wait in the car while the black man speaks with a guy who is waiting around the plane. They see him flash a bank roll and give the guy some money and then comes back to the car. This is odd because he'd told them he had no money. He motions them out of the car.

'It's all fueled up and ready to go,' he said to them. 'Here is all the information you need to land it on a dirt strip in the jungle of Belize.' He gives them a package, gets in his car and drives away.

"And that's it?" Barkow demanded.

"Yes. They landed as instructed and were met by a guy in a jeep who drove them out of the jungle and told them never to talk about the plane again."

"Great," Barkow said. "I want to talk to those two men."

"No can do. Chico and Nat swore me to secrecy and told me this story over a month ago and I have not seen either of them since. It is very odd because I have known both for a long time and they are regular customers."

"How can I find that dirt strip?"

"They said they were given a GPS location and that is how they found it to land. The jeep ride took many jungle trails coming out and they were warned to tell no one of how they flew a Lancair back to Belize."

"Then why did they tell you?"

"We are old friends who grew up together. We were having a three-way party and were pretty drunk on the night they told me."

"And you have not seen them for three weeks?"

"That is correct and I'm worried. In fact, I'm taking what you pay me and leaving Belize. Something big is going down and I don't want to go with it."

"Has anyone else asked you anything about the Lancair?"

"No, only you."

"Why is your brother and his friend so interested in you?"

"They are guarding me. We are all three leaving Belize. I advise you to do the same. Things have not been the same around here since an abundance of drugs began showing up on the streets, controlled by a very tough crowd."

"I want the name of a local bush pilot who makes frequent trips to jungle villages."

"That would be Lisandro Vito. He knows every village in Belize and flies supplies to them all the time."

"How do I find Lisandro?"

"He hangs at a bar called *The Hanger* and goes by the name of Vito."

Barkow picked up the money from the dash and gave it all to Rosita.

"Thanks, Rosie. I think it's wise of you to get out right away. Something big is taking place here. Someone reached out to me in the States, advising me not to come to Belize. It was a delaying tactic to keep me away."

"Thanks for the money Barkow. We leave tomorrow on the ferry, but you can share my bed tonight, no charge."

"Sorry, Rosie, but tonight I have other fish to fry. I wish you a safe journey."

Rosita leaned over and brushed her lips over Barkow's cheek then slipped out of the car and returned to *The Palms*. Barkow backed the Explorer out of the parking slot and headed back to the trendy part of Belize City, to search for Lisandro Vito.

CHAPTER FIVE

THE NEXT MORNING after breakfast, Barkow resumed his search for Lisandro Vito and found him at a small booth signed *Vito's Express Flights*, in the Tourism Village.

"Hello, are you Vito?" He said.

"Yes. I am Vito. May I be of service?"

"Perhaps, do you take passengers as well as freight?"

"Yes, I do scenic flights."

"Are you free to give a flight today?"

"Today I work in the booth. What do you have in mind?"

"Today I will pay double for a flight that may take all day."

"Where is the destination?"

"I don't know. I'm searching for a remote dirt landing strip in the jungle."

"This is a big country, my friend, with a lot of jungle."

"I have a Landing-strip-finder, it gives me an advantage."

"That would be a handy piece of equipment. What does it look like?"

"It looks exactly like a big chunk of cold, hard cash."

"How big?"

"That all depends on how quickly I locate the correct strip," Barkow said.

"If you were to be standing on that strip by noon today—how much?"

"If that were the case I could pay ten large, when I am returned here."

Vito's head turned back and forth as he searched for suspicious looking characters who may be watching. Satisfied, he turned back to Barkow.

"Rosita gave me a call last night and said you may be coming to see me."

"Then you know what I am looking for. Do we have a deal?"

"Come back here in one hour. I will close up and be ready to go.

"See you in an hour," Barkow said and walked away.

⊙ The helicopter lifted from the pad to an altitude of 700 feet and then headed west. The town appeared to quickly slide away behind them as they flew arrow-straight, locked on a single course. Barkow looked as they sped past the jungle. They crossed over streams and a few dirt roads showing through the foliage at times. Before long the jungle thinned as swamps took over the terrain showing dead trees, standing in swamp water at odd angles. Upon green mounds scattered throughout the swamps, the jungle vegetation grew, densely crowded together on any ground rising above the surface of the swamp. The mounds were inhabited only by birds and monkeys. Eventually they shot over a larger jungle-covered area like a green island in the endless swamps.

We flew in a straight line from Belize City to this place so it's obvious the pilot has been here before. He knew exactly what course brought him directly to this particular location, perhaps having been here many times in the past. Barkow's thinking was interrupted when the pilot's voice sounded loud and clearly over his headphones.

"Can you see that streak through the jungle below where the vegetation is not as high or thick as the rest of the area?"

"Yeah, it's obvious when you point it out. What caused it?"

"A few months ago that strip was cleared of vegetation by hand-axe and saw. The ground was leveled and packed by the hundreds, if not thousands, of Indians who did the work, then vanished into the jungle."

"How do you happen to know about this event taking place?"

"About once a month I bring supplies to villages near the ancient ruins of Lamanai and Chan Chich near the Guatemala border. My course of flight brings me directly over this location."

"You said the Indians vanished. Where did they go?"

"I have no idea. I come this way about every thirty days. I first saw them starting to clear the land, the next time it was almost a finished cleared strip of raw land with many Indians swarming everywhere. From then on it was deserted with the jungle reclaiming it. In another month or two it will be so overgrown I will not be able to ever land here again. This is the only thing I have to offer for that which you seek."

"Okay. Thanks for the information. Let's set down and have a look around."

"Roger that."

The helicopter made a banking turn and began following the strip until the pilot selected a place of tall grass and small bushes. He hovered over his chosen location and slowly lowered until the landing struts dropped into four foot high savanna grass and settled on solid ground. When the blades stopped rotating Barkow threw open his door and looked out.

"Good Lord," Barkow exclaimed. "The grass blades reach half way up the copter door".

"I know. The jungle heals itself quite quickly. I will remain in the copter and you can look around all you want, but only for the length of four hours. At that time, with or without you, this bird leaves the jungle and returns to Belize City."

"I understand. I'll be back as soon as I have a look around."

Barkow stepped out of the copter and dropped into the grass. He checked his watch and studied the angle of the sun. He struck out moving in an easterly direction, wading through the shoulder high vegetation, around huge fern and broadleaf plants. He headed toward older trees with higher growth marking the edge of the strip. He'd estimated the total strip length to be 2,500 feet.

When he reached the edge of the taller trees he found the foliage not so dense beneath them. He began making his way in a northerly direction through fern-trees and tropical plants, staying close to the edge of the grass infested strip. Not far from where he'd turned north, Barkow came upon the tumbled down remains of a shack made of poles. Dead palm fronds, probably the roof, covered most of the rubble that was once a crude building. He prowled around, poking here and there but found nothing of interest. Moving farther back into the trees a jumble of vines climbing in confusion over what he thought may be a fallen tree with some remaining limbs protruding upwards. When moving on he noticed a red smudge behind some of the tangled creepers. He went closer to pull a few clinging vines away and discovered an iron framework with places showing a covering of moldy, reddish leather.

I know what this is, he thought to himself and began ripping and pulling away more of the creeping plant. *The Lancair had red leather upholstery in the interior. This is what's left of the seat frames and cushions.*

Further investigation revealed some corroded metal parts with a fake wood finish and chrome knobs. A large metal object in the moldy leaves proved to the forward landing gear with wheel still attached. Prowling around through the undergrowth, he came across both of the rear landing gears complete with wheels. A picture formed in Barkow's mind.

The Lancair was brought here and had its interior stripped out, but why? Why steal an expensive plane like this and tear it apart? Why take the landing gear off. Because— the thought flashed in his brain—*they want to put on pontoons and use it for a cargo plane. Then why not steal a plane with pontoons on it already? Maybe haul drugs or something. It's small, light and fast and I'll bet it is going to have a special use for whoever has gone to this much trouble.*

"That's it. That's why." he suddenly said aloud.

He at once started back to the copter. As he climbed in

his seat the pilot hit the starter and the blades began to rotate, picking up speed.

"That didn't take long. Did you find anything of importance?"

"Is there a river somewhere close by here?" Barkow said.

"We're in the Cockscomb Basin. It covers over 100,000 acres of jungles, mountains and swamps; It's the world's only jaguar reserve with many rivers and streams. What kind do you have in mind?"

"One that is close, long, fairly flat and runs year round," Barkow said with a crooked smile.

"We'll go up and look around this location and see if any of them suit you."

The helicopter lifted out of the grass and rose to 500 feet then began to circle around the area. The headphones crackled in the pilot's ear.

"The river I want needs to be close to the strip we just left, have a straight run for at least 1,500 feet and flow year round. It needs to be from 30 to 50 feet wide."

The pilot gave a thumbs-up sign and increased the width of the searching circle course. Suddenly he lowered the speed and dropped to skim across a lagoon at tree-top level. Below them Barkow could make out places where filtered light reflected off water. Palms and fern trees reached out over the water and nearly camouflaged both lagoon and a widening river flowing away in a relatively straight westerly course.

"I think this is good for now." He barked into the head-set microphone. "Get the coordinates of this location and take me back to Belize City."

The copter rose as it banked away on a new heading and eventually settled down on its landing pad in Belize City. When they exited the helicopter, Vito said to his passenger. "Come to the office and I'll buy you a drink."

"Sounds good." Barkow said.

In the small office Vito poured tequila into ice filled glasses and offered one to Barkow.

"Salud." Barkow said. They touched glasses and each took a sip. Barkow removed the proper amount of payment from his wallet and set the cash on the edge of Vito's desk.

"I'll need your services again tomorrow at sunrise, if you're available?"

"I'll have the bird ready for takeoff when you arrive." Vito said as his cell phone sounded an incoming call.

"Hola… Que?... Rosita?" he uttered. "Por que?"

"Sounds like a problem." Barkow said.

Vito rattled off a string of excited Spanish and cut the connection.

"Yes, it is a very severe problem. Rosita, her brother and another man were found, with their throats cut, at the ferry dock last night. It is now a time for extreme caution."

"Damn it!" Barkow growled. "Rosie didn't get out in time. Tell me Vito. Do you know a man who can speak English, knows his way around the jungle and is not afraid of danger?"

"I know such a man, but I cannot give you his name because that would cost me my life. I can only see to it that he has your name and contact number. He will call you if he is interested in a proposition."

"That's satisfactory. Please convey it is extremely urgent and I would require his assistance for perhaps several days. The job would start tomorrow at sunrise."

"I can do that."

"Good. Be prepared to carry one or two passenger's tomorrow morning, because either way, he goes with me or I go alone. All you need do is take me to that overgrown strip in the jungle and return home."

Barkow shook Vito's hand and drove to the Tourism Village. He found an outfitters store and purchased among other things a small backpack, a pair of jungle boots, bush clothing, headgear and a bowie knife with sheath. From there he went to a store that specialized in electronic surveillance equipment.

Back in his hotel room, Barkow shaved, showered and called Laura on the satellite phone.

"Hello Barkow, I miss you."

"Hi Laura, I miss you too. The sound of your voice is like a bit of heaven. Is everything alright?"

"It's fine here. I have heard nothing from those horrid street gangs who'd kidnapped me."

"That's the way it's supposed to be. You must be all settled in the condo now. Any questions?"

"Nope. You have a lovely apartment; very exclusive. Jim Greenwell called and asked if there was anything I needed. I also had a call from Blanco who said to tell you that Juan was back with the Dogs and all is quiet on the home front."

"Sounds like everything is under control. Wish I was with you."

"No, I wish I was with you. There you are in a tropical paradise and I'm alone in sunny Arizona. How are things going?"

"I have a few leads and think I'll score big in the next day or two. If Goodfellow calls tell him I'm making progress. Oops, my cell is buzzing. Gotta go."

"Will do. Take care of yourself and don't forget who loves you."

"That's something I'll never forget. I love you too, ya know."

"Goodbye, Barkow, hurry home."

"Goodbye, Laura, I'll be there quick as I can."

Barkow turned off the satellite phone and answered his cell. "Barkow." He said.

"What you want Jungle Man for?" a female voice said.

"What I want is a man who knows the ways of the jungle and can handle himself with the natives."

"Jungle Man knows his jungle."

"What is his name?"

"Just call him Jungle Man"

"Okay. Can he start tomorrow?

"He is ready now."

"Does he have a gun I can borrow for a few days?"

"How much you pay?"

"I pay one thousand American dollars per day."

"He has a gun."

"Tell him to bring the gun and bullets. Be at Vito's helicopter pad, sunrise tomorrow. We go into jungle."

"Jungle Man will be there."

The cell phone went silent.

CHAPTER SIX

BARKOW ARRIVED AT *Vito's Express Flights* in the dark, pre-dawn hours. A feeling of unease that haunted him through the night was still present. He cut the headlights prior to turning into the industrial complex and parked in the dark shadows of a building adjacent to Vito's shop. Leaving the car, he drifted silently through the darkness; a black phantom following a perimeter course around and behind the pad where the helicopter stood and Vito's office. Barkow stopped at the building's corner and stood immobile in dark shadows. He let his gaze slowly search the grounds around the building; a warning clicked in his mind... *Wait. Something is different.* He flicked his attention back over the path his visual search had previously taken and studied the dark scenes he had just looked at. *There,* he thought. *Between the door and window of the office is something to some degree different. A black mass against a black background.*

The difference between one shadow placed upon another was something that perhaps one man in a thousand could have noticed. Barkow was that one man. Having been, for six years, a covert killer for the Army, he had been specifically trained by experts to rely on his senses. A somber melody creeping into his mind was ignored as his hand slowly slipped, inch by inch, to caress the crosshatched handle of the bowie knife strapped to his left thigh. He moved silently from shadow to shadow as he retraced his route back around the building and appeared at the opposite corner but closer to that slight difference of colored darkness.

"Good morning, Barkow." Announced a soft, low voice.

"Good morning, Jungle man." Barkow said, equally low, then glided over to settle beside him.

The magical quality of false dawn soon transformed the inky blackness, degree by degree, causing the image of the jungle guide to gradually appear against the building wall. He was shorter than five feet in height and wore only a breechcloth and a knife. His black hair was tied with a leather thong at the back of his head. Also secured to each arm, above the bicep, were simple rawhide thongs with 6 inch tails dangling loosely from the knot. He retrieved an item from a backpack and shoved a revolver, holstered in a loaded cartridge belt, over to Barkow.

"Return when leave Belize," He said.

The Sun rose above the horizon and with it Vito's helicopter containing the pilot and two passengers. As the aircraft banked above its landing pad Barkow saw a man in a bush hat standing beside a jeep, looking up. The pilot came out of the banking turn and made a straight bee-line flight to the location of the nearly overgrown strip that had been recently hand-hacked from the living jungle.

Looking down on the new growth of vegetation as they began their decent, Barkow's thoughts massaged the situation: *This strip was cut out of the jungle for the single purpose of one plane making one landing. It was a huge and costly undertaking for some unknown purpose. Indians did the work according to Vito. Why would anyone want to put an expensive airplane into the jungle? It was obviously stripped here and moved elsewhere. Who is the man by the jeep when we departed Belize?*

The downwash from the copter blades made the tall bush grass wildly swirl and weave, as the landing struts settled into their midst.

"Thanks Vito. I have a satellite phone with me and will call when and if we need to be picked up. You've been a big help."

Vito gave a thumbs-up sign and the two passengers slipped out the door and ducked beneath the slow rotating blades to vanish into the tall jungle grass. The copter lifted and veered away while they made their way over to the taller trees and worked north to the site where Barkow had seen the stripped parts of the Lancair. Barkow showed the Jungle Man the various things he had found and then led him along the strip to its northern end where the taller tree limbs closed together, blocking out most sunlight. Barkow spoke to his companion who seemed completely at ease moving through the tangled vegetation.

"Tell me, Jungle Man, by what name do your friends call you."

"Me, Conchaco."

"Okay," Barkow said. "I'll call you Con, if that's alright."

"Con, okay."

"Alright Con, we are searching for a trail, cut through the jungle, probably to a river that is north of here."

"Old trail?"

"Yeah, maybe about a month ago."

"Trail for?"

"Thirty feet wide to carry a plane to the river."

"I find trail."

With that said, Conchaco walked to the right about fifty feet then moved north and walked to his left the same distance. Then he moved north and reversed the walk. This he did several times until he stopped at a large tree fern.

"Here trail."

Barkow looked at the foliage all around that seemed the same in all directions.

"I see no trail."

"Barkow look, no see," Con said. "Here more light."

He stood facing north and raised both arms above his head, then dropped them to shoulder height, pointing both northward.

"More light."

He turned, pointing both arms east.

"Less light."

He turned again pointing west.

"Less light."

Con moved closer to the tree fern and swept back the

long overlaying fronds that reached out with their tips almost touching the ground. Sticking up out of the dead compost of twigs and decaying matter beneath the fern were several short dead stalks.

"Fern no let sun through. All below die. Look at stalk."

The dead stalks were 8 to 12 inches high and had their tops cut off at a smooth angle.

"Machete cut jungle… make trail."

"Conchaco is a good jungle man." Barkow said. "I could never have found this trail."

A hint of smile touched the short Mayan's lips as he turned and strode northward through tangled foliage. Strange chirps, snorts and calls from the jungle's inhabitants created a bedlam of sound. The air was muggy but not uncomfortable as they made their way following a route that Barkow was certain the Lancair had been carried. In a shadowed vale Con whistled an odd call. Eechoo-eechoo-eechoo.

The answering echo came back. Eechoo-eechoo-eechoo.

"Yellow head water bird," he muttered.

"I only know one bird call," Barkow said. He whistled one of the most distinctive calls of the Blue Jay, often referred to as the "rusty pump" call, so named because it sounded just like the squeaky resemblance to the screech of an old fashioned, hand-operated, water pump that had rusted out. Con mimicked the call precisely.

Sometime later Con stopped and held his hand up. Turning back to Barkow he placed his finger across his lips in the universal sign to remain silent. They stood motionless; birds called; insects buzzed; a troop of monkeys swung effortlessly through the treetops. Con signaled Barkow to remain, then turned and disappeared into the tangled vines and creepers of the flora. Minutes of time slowly passed; the sounds of the jungle continued its normal routine.

Con reappeared and motioned Barkow to follow. They made their way forward for about thirty yards and stopped. Con spread aside the huge leaves of an elephant ear plant and Barkow realized they were standing on the muddy edge of a slough. Along the bank of the bog pond leading off to their right, giant tree fern and palm trees leaned over the water.

"Go this way," Con said as he turned to walk directly away from the lagoon.

"Is this where the trail ends?" Barkow said.

"Trail go along water's edge."

"Then why go this way?"

"Ko-rock," Con said as he continued moving away from the water.

Barkow stopped. "Wait up," he called. Con was soon out of sight among the jungle foliage. Barkow turned and started back to the lagoon. He had no intention of leaving that faintly outlined trail. Retracing their path he pushed aside a plant with large leaves and suddenly stood face to face... with Con.

"What the hell," He cursed. "How'd you get here? You'll have to stop appearing like that."

"Come," Con said.

He selected a tree with huge, twisting limbs growing from the trunk in all directions and began climbing upwards. Barkow followed.

The tree was quite tall and soon they were in the upper canopy of the forest. When Con stopped, so did Barkow.

"Look," the Mayan said, pointing toward a glimpse of the water where they had previously stood looking at the lagoon. Just beyond, the jungle growth thinned slightly. Splotches of sun fell upon sparse, dark grass and half buried gray logs that lay haphazardly scattered in the grass.

"Yeah, I see. So what?"

"Ko-rock... go 'round."

Barkow studied the clearing, water and plants more closely, then suddenly breathed the words. "My God, crocodiles."

The reptiles were dozing in the semi clearing. While Barkow and Con watched, one slowly dragged its great body through the grassy mud and slid silently into the water. *I would have walked right into them*, Barkow thought, as he climbed down from the tree.

"Okay Con. You lead, I follow."

The Mayan said nothing, but stared at Barkow and slowly nodded his head, then turned and walked away. Barkow followed.

They circled around the crocodiles and returned to the edge of the lagoon. The foliage grew so thick at the edge of the water they could not get close. Once more they moved away from the lagoon going in a northwest direction until they came to a stream. They were following the stream back to the lagoon when Con stopped. He gave the silence sign to Barkow and indicated for him to wait, then disappeared into the bush.

The minutes crawled by. Barkow sat on the bank of the stream and withdrew the weapon he'd borrowed from the guide. Having been well schooled in firearms, he recognized it as a Dan Wesson Model 715 – .357 Magnum. It was designed and built to be the most accurate, rugged and versatile revolver on the market. It had a 6" barrel with a heavy vent-shroud profile to tame the .357's recoil.

The scabbard and ammunition belt was custom made for the gun to hang low, strapped to the thigh. There was a leather safety thong on the holster that tied the revolver in place.

I couldn't have picked a better weapon if I had my choice, he thought as he slid the gun back into its leather holster. The Bowie knife was strapped to his left thigh. It had a special sheath with a built on pocket for a whetstone. Barkow pulled both knife and pre-oiled stone from the sheath and began gently drawing the blade across the flat surface. Over two hours passed before Con returned.

"Welcome back," Barkow said.

"Trail end at ko-rock where airplane go water. This river come out lagoon where two native with one canoe, wait.

CHAPTER SEVEN

"**G**OOD JOB, CON," Barkow said as he mulled the situation over. He removed his backpack, checked the contents and took a small electronic device from the pack. He slipped the device into a pouch-pocket of his jungle jeans as he turned over questions in his mind.

If the Lancair was put into the water at the lagoon it was probably headed for the river that flows westerly, but why? If the two Indians wait to see if anyone follows, they will probably use the single canoe to go and warn someone, but who? The answer to that is whoever wants to use that Lancair for something, but why out here in a jungle swamp? I have to get a tracking device on that canoe....

His thoughts faded into unanswered murkiness and he abruptly turned his attention to a plan of action.

"Okay, Con," he said. "Can you create a diversion to lure those two Indians away from their canoe for a few minutes?"

"They know jungle. Difficult get both away."

"I need five minutes alone with the canoe."

"Okay, Con draw Indian away.

"How will you do that?"

"I go first we find trail. Shoot gun one time, boom. Count all fingers, shoot gun three time, boom, boom, boom."

"Then what?"

"Mayan warrior come, hurry-hurry. I lead away through swamp. Meet here."

"How long will you be gone," Barkow said.

Con spread his hands before him and hunched his shoulders

with an 'I don't know' sign. He pointed at Barkow and said; "Go climb look-look ko-rock tree."

"Why do that?"

"Maya Indian plenty smart. Barkow hide. When hear bang, bang, bang. Wait five minute, go canoe hurry, hurry, came back wait for Con."

"Are you sure it will work?"

"It work." He said as he solemnly nodded his head.

Barkow unstrapped and unbuckled the gun belt with holstered firearm and handed it to Con. The Mayan guide buckled the belt together and hung it over one shoulder, letting the heavy weapon hang under the opposite armpit.

"Good luck Con," Barkow said.

With a nod, the jungle man vanished into the forest.

Barkow made his way back to the tree from which Con had shown him the crocodiles. He climbed high into the canopy of the trees where he could not see the jungle floor below. He chose a location directly above a section of the trunk where a heavy group of limbs jutted out close together below him. He hung his backpack on a limb and dug out a length of nylon rope. With a few deft twists and knots he fashioned a snipers sling where he could swing in comparative comfort as he waited for the signal of three shots. An energy bar and a drink of water created lunch.

Dozing in the warmth of the upper reaches, he abruptly snapped awake at the sound of a far off shot. Without thinking he mentally counted off ten fingers and right on cue, boom-boom-boom. He checked his watch and five minutes later began to slip down limb to limb, descending the tree.

He found the river and followed it to where it flowed out of the lagoon. The canoe was tied off to a tree with a twist of vine. On the ground below the knotted vine was a three inch wooden spike, worn smooth, with a strange idol's head carved on the end opposite the point. Barkow slipped it into his pocket and studied the canoe. It was a two man craft made of the burned out center of a tree trunk. It was shallow and flat bottomed with squared off ends. The burned out cavity was scraped clean of charcoal and the entire hull had been shaped with some sort of adz. A long, slender pole and two short, carved paddles lay in the boat.

Barkow removed the signal sender's envelope from his pocket and tore it open. He set the tiny sensor to transmit to the GPS device in his backpack. The envelope included a small nail, a screw and a tiny tube of waterproof superglue. He pushed the nail through the provided hole in the sender and forced it into the dugout's stern, below the lip and above the waterline. Then, making sure he had all the scraps of packaging from the unit in his pocket and had left no tell-tale tracks, returned to his treetop retreat. He approached the tree slowly and carefully inspected the area for signs of anyone having been there. Limb by limb he climbed upwards through the structure of the huge tree to his sniper's sling.

He removed the GPS unit, turned on the power and hit search. The screen lit up and a map of Belize appeared with a tiny, blinking green light. Displayed across the bottom of the screen was the lat/long position. The sender was working perfectly.

When the afternoon faded into dusk, the bird calls quieted as a new set of night sounds began and Barkow drifted into sleep. He awoke when something crashed through the shrubbery below. A sound of half snarl, half growl was heard as something in pursuit followed. The silence returned and unanswered questions in his mind resurfaced.

It could have been one of the jaguars or other cats Con told me about. I wonder how he made out with the Indians. Where did they take the plane? They hauled the damn thing weighing thousands of pounds through the jungle from the strip to this lagoon. Maybe they put it on a raft. Why are two Indians waiting here? Are they meeting someone? There's no way that canoe can hold three people. In the solitude of thought a warning note pinged in his mind.

The slight sound of a tree limb that creaked under a weight being placed on it brought instant disregard of his thoughts as all Barkow's senses were now directed on that single breath of sound. His hand slid to the crosshatched handle of the Bowie knife at his left thigh and slowly withdrew the razor-sharp blade from its sheath.

A movement of air rippled the leaves in a faint rustling sound. Without conscious thought Barkow knew that whoever was climbing the tree below him would have to gain the distance equal to his height in the tree to obtain striking distance because of the thick growth of branches directly below him. He sensed, rather than heard the slow upward progress. With the Bowie knife in hand, Barkow waited, calm, confident and ready.

In the quiet solitude of the night a clear sound of Blue Jay with perfect emphasis on the squeaky syllable brought relief of tension and a smile to Barkow's lips.

That's the rusty pump call of Blue Jay, he thought, *I taught it to Con when he whistled the call of the yellow crowned night-heron for me.*

He answered with a similar call and heard a scrambling up through the limbs.

"Welcome home, Con. Where are the Indians?"

"They on false trail through swamp."

"I have the canoe rigged so we can go back to the strip at first light."

"Better wait, they come back." Con said as he handed the gun-belt with revolver to Barkow.

Dawn broke and with it came the incessant calling, chirping and hooting sounds of morning in the jungle. Con watched Barkow as he pulled a wooden item from his pocket.

"Here's something I found by the canoe." Barkow said as he handed him the worn, pointed shaft carved with an idol head on one end.

"Is Aztec god," Con said. "It hair keeper; push through hair-knot, keep tied."

"I thought these Indians were Mayan, not Aztec."

"This bad omen," Con muttered.

CHAPTER EIGHT

BARKOW BROUGHT THE GPS out of his backpack and checked the blinking green signal. It was moving slowly westward.

"They're on the move Con, so we can head back to the strip. I'll call Vito to pick us up."

They collected their gear and were soon on the way back to the location where the helicopter had brought them. When they arrived they sat in the shade of a broad-leaf tree, waiting for Vito to come in.

"When we get back to Belize City I'll pay you." Barkow said. "It may be a day or two but I want to hire you again as soon as I find out where the canoe went."

The jungle guide looked directly into Barkow's eyes and nodded his head. He was a man of few words.

"What can you tell me about the Aztec carving I found?"

"It Tonatuih, sun god five." He held up his open hand and touched the thumb and each of the four fingers with his other index finger. "Aztec gods no easy explain. Tonatuih last sun god."

"Why were there five sun gods?"

"Sun god make sun go through sky. Five worlds, five gods."

"Why were there five worlds?"

"Each world have one sun god. All worlds die. We world five."

"Who is our sun god?

"No more sun god."

"Why not?"

"You no learn in many lifetimes."

The Mayan guide stood up and vanished into the jungle without another word.

That's odd, Barkow thought. *Maybe I made him mad asking about the Aztecs. When I get back to my hotel I need to call Laura and Harry. I also need to check out that guy in the bush hat that keeps popping up.*

When Vito arrived in the helicopter, Con had not returned. Barkow gathered his gear and struck out through the tall savanna grass, arriving at the aircraft the same time Con came to it from a different direction. They ducked under the rotating blades and entered the passenger compartment, buckled in and put on the headphones.

"Did you find what you searched for?" Vito's voice crackled over the headset.

"The trip was very productive." Barkow answered.

No more was said until the craft settled upon its landing pad. They disembarked and Barkow took Con to one side. He counted out the agreed upon payment and handed it to the guide.

"Here's your payment. I will need you in a day or two when we return to the jungle. You know how to take care of yourself and are a good companion. I consider you my friend."

Barkow extended his arm for a handshake. The short Mayan looked into Barkow's eyes for a long moment, then thrust his hand into the outstretched hand before him. One time they pumped up then down and Con released the handshake.

"Barkow, Con, now friend." He held the money out to Barkow. "Con no take money from friend."

"No." Barkow said. "It is a gift. Please take the gift from friend to friend."

Con, still holding the money out, slowly nodded his head. "Barkow call when go jungle." He said, turned and walked away.

"I'll call, Con." Barkow said after him.

"I'll need your bird again in a few days, Vito."

"You are moving very quickly, my friend." Vito said. "This is a time for you to be extremely cautious. I have received a message warning me of the risk I take doing business with you."

"What have you decided to do?"

"No one tells Vito who he can or cannot do business with, but I now carry a sidearm at all times. We are living in the time of great danger. I see a very bad situation developing on the streets and in the casinos.

"Thanks Vito. I think things will move quickly in the next few days. Keep a sharp lookout and take care of yourself."

Barkow drove back to his hotel, parked in back and went straight to the hotel lounge. From a darkened corner table he ordered bourbon on the rocks. From this location he could see across the lounge and through the door to the hotel check-in desk. He finished his drink and walked to the door between the lounge and the lobby. He saw in the corner of the lobby a tall man seated in an easy chair with a side table. On the table was a bush hat. When a customer came into the lobby the tall man studied him and Barkow, seeing his chance, left the lounge unnoticed and went to his room. He shaved and took a shower, than lay on the bed and slept for two hours. He had the knack of being able to sleep for a predetermined time and wake up. It was like a built-in alarm clock. He drew the drapes and turned out the lights in his room. Stepping to the darkened drapes he carefully pulled them aside and stared at the parking lot. His instincts were correct, a shadow moves among the parked cars.

Barkow opened his door to the hall and checked both directions, then stepped into the passageway, went down the back stairway and stopped at the side door to the parking lot. He stood inside looking out the door window for a length of time until he noticed a movement along the second row of parked cars. A shadow slid among the cars and stopped at his rented Ford Explorer. In a moment the driver's door opened and the curtsey light flashed on and was extinguished at once.

Someone is checking out my car, he thought, *it could be that guy in the bush hat.*

He walked back to the lobby and out the front door. Following a sidewalk along the side of the building, with all senses alert, he headed for the parking lot and straight to his car. A shadow slithered out the row of cars and vanished into the shrubbery along the back of the building. Barkow acted as if he'd left something in the car which he came to retrieve. He then walked back toward the front entrance of the hotel. As he approached the building he saw the shadow slip through the shrubs and around the corner. A smile, devoid of humor, creased his lips for an instant.

Someone who is not very good at the spying business, is doing their best to keep up with where I go, who I see and what I do. They're going to find out this is not a game for rookies.

He kept walking, turned the corner and continued along the front side of the building toward the entrance. As the light from the entrance increased, Barkow saw a tall man and a woman in an embrace. They looked like a statue as he held her leaning back with his lips close to hers, but not touching. They held that position until he walked past as though he didn't see them. He turned into the hotel and went straight into the lounge, taking his previous seat.

He watched as the tall man in the bush hat came in looking around and went to the check-in counter. He had a few words with the desk clerk who answered and gave a nod of his head toward the door of the lounge. The tall man took a comfortable seat in the lobby and opened a newspaper. Barkow opened the door and went into the lobby and over to the elevator. He arrived at his second story room and went in. He turned the lights on, waited five minutes and turned them off. He slipped into to the hallway, down the back stairs and out the door to the parking lot. He stepped into the shrubbery growing along the building's side, waited and watched. After ten minutes he crept along the wall to the corner and peered around it. Close to the hotel entrance stood the man in the bush hat. The woman, his accomplice, was nowhere to be seen.

He let his gaze slowly search the grounds around the building; a warning clicked in his mind. *Stop and listen. Make sure no one is around.* Satisfied, he continued moving deliberately and silent until he was within arm's reach of the tall man and stopped. *This poor schmuck doesn't have a clue,* he thought.

Sudden as the strike of a rattlesnake, Barkow's left arm shot out; his hand closed over both mouth and nose of the tall man, pulling his head sideways and down into a headlock from his right arm, using his weight to bring the target to a crumpled position on the ground. A quick judo punch on a precise location of a nerve in the man's neck paralyzed him for the time being while duct tape covered his mouth and tie-ties secured his hands behind his back.

CHAPTER NINE

A FEW BLOCKS DOWN from the Radisson Hotel was a vacant building, wedged between the New Belize Tourist Information Company and a Real Estate office. In the back room of this empty building is where the tall man, minus bush hat, is secured to an old office chair. His wrists are lashed to the armrests and ankles to the revolving assembly of the wheeled legs. His torso is tightly tied to the chair back.

The numbing effect of being nerve-punched was wearing off and he began to struggle against his restraints as he turned his head back and forth trying to make out where he was. Barkow, unseen in the darkness, stood before him.

"It will do no good to struggle," he said. "I know how to tie a man to a chair and it will simply result in pain if you try to escape.

With an aching head and a dizzy feeling the man spoke to the sound of the voice.

"Where am I?"

"You're right where I want you to be." Barkow said.

"What do you want of me?"

"I want to know three things. Who you are, what you do in Belize and why you're following me around."

"I'm Hector Madoff. I'm working for the Belize City Police and I'm keeping track of what you do and where you go."

"Okay, Hector. What do you do for the Police?"

"I'm an informant."

"A snitch, eh?"

"That's a crude reference, but yes, I sell them information."

"Tell me, Hector, when did they put you on my tail?"

"They did not, Sir. I was at the airport when you came in and thought you may be an interesting subject to observe."

"You just picked me out of the blue to follow around?"

"That is correct."

"The cops don't know you're doing this surveillance?"

"No, Sir. They do not."

"Then why the hell did you pick me to follow?"

"Because, Sir, you did not seem to be a tourist, but you appeared to be here for a specific reason and you don't look like a businessman."

"So, Hector, you hang out at the airport and follow people around in the hope something will turn up that you can sell to the police."

"Sir, these are very dangerous times in Belize. Someone is flooding the population with drugs at a cut-rate price. Strange men are using strong-arm tactics against some businesses and people are being killed in back alleys. I love my country and I will help the police in any way I am able."

"Who's the Broad?"

"The what?"

"The broad, the dame, that skirt you were pretending to kiss tonight?"

"Oh! That's Roni, she rents a room from me. Her name is Veronica Lowen and she works at a law office here in the city. She left her house key in the office and it was locked up so she called to ask if she could borrow mine until tomorrow. I was very surprised when you walked by and could only think to pretend we were a couple out for a stroll.

Barkow took out his jack knife and Hector's eyes grew wide.

"Listen, Hector, you've got the dumbest way of helping the police I've ever heard of."

He cut the bonds from Hector's wrists, torso and ankles.

"You can get yourself killed following strangers around."

"With all this crime going on, this is the only way I can think of to be of some assistance to my country."

"Find a new way to help and don't follow me anymore." Barkow's gaze held Hector's rapt attention a moment, then he turned and walked out of the building, going toward to his hotel.

So Hector is just a police informant, he thought as he walked in the warm night air. *Bullshit! That's a pack of lies if I ever heard any. I need to know the truth about what's going down.*

At the end of the block he suddenly veered into the shrubs at the side of the walk and turned his gaze back upon the building he had just left. Hector, soon came out looking both ways and walked rapidly toward the Radisson Hotel. Barkow let him pass and fell in behind to see where he went. At the guest parking lot he got in a dark sedan and pulled out of the lot. He never saw the Ford Explorer that followed a block behind with headlights off.

Hector drove across town and parked near what appeared to be a small city park. He left the car and followed a curving, shadowed walkway beneath the trees. He came to a clearing with children's swings, a teeter-totter and a slide with park benches scattered around. A woman sat on a bench in the darkness. He went directly to her.

"Hi, Hector," she said. "How did it go?"

"That man scared the devil out of me, Roni. I thought he was going to kill me for sure."

"What happened after I left?"

"I was watching the front door like you said to do, and all of a sudden there he was, right beside me. I never heard a thing until he grabbed me by my throat and forced me to the ground.

"Oh my God," she exclaimed. "Did he hurt you?"

"He hit a nerve or something on my neck and I couldn't move my legs, then I passed out."

"Oh, Hector." She reached out and touched his shoulder. "I never should have asked you to watch him for me."

"That's not all. He took me to a vacant building and tied me to a chair and was questioning me. I made up a silly story and eventually he let me go. I almost wet my pants, I was so scared."

"I'm so sorry, Hector. Don't watch him anymore. Go home now."

"He wanted to know who you are."

"What did you say?"

"I made up a lie about you needing to borrow a house key and he bought it. Then he let me go."

"Okay. You go on home Hector and I'll see you later. I feel so badly about getting you in trouble."

"It's okay Roni. I'll be fine. See you later."

"Bye, Hector."

Hector hurried away and Roni dug out her cell phone.

"Hi. It's me…. No, nothing yet…. How should I know? We have to let it unfold…. No, absolutely not. I don't want you messing it up. Just wait a few more days. Something's going to pop soon. I can feel it in my bones…. Yeah, bye."

Roni sat on the bench, absently holding her phone and thinking. A minute later she gathered up her purse and dropped the phone inside just as a man stepped from the shadows.

"Hello, Roni. We have things to discuss," Barkow said.

Her first reaction was to stand up. He placed a hand on each shoulder and forced her to remain on the bench.

"Sit, Roni. I have no intention to hurt you unless you refuse to answer a few questions."

"What do you want?"

"Honest answers."

"About what?"

"Why do you have Hector watching me?"

"Hector is doing me a favor."

"That little favor almost cost Hector his life."

"He is no threat. Why would you want to harm Hector?"

"A deadly game of cat and mouse is being played in this community. People are being killed. I don't' want to be one of them. Who're you talking with on the phone?"

"That's no concern of yours."

He reached out and grabbed her arm in a vice-like grip.

"Are you stupid, Roni? Do you want to be hurt? I do not have the luxury of time to waste."

"My name is Veronica Lowen. I'm a Reporter for the International Times," she said, "based in San Francisco."

"What're you doing in Belize?"

"I'm trying to uncover the reason for the influx of crime here."

"Who'd you talk to on the phone?"

"He's my partner. A fellow Reporter."

"What's his name and where's he at?"

"I'm not at liberty to say."

"Listen to me, Miss Lowen." He relaxed and touched her shoulder. "I don't want to hurt you. This city, maybe this whole country, is in a state of instability. Crime is on the rise and people are being murdered. The best thing you can do is get on the next flight out of here and go back to San Francisco. Now, what's his name and where's he at?"

"His name is Gary Appelton and he's in a hotel near here."

"Alright Roni, now why are you following me."

"Because you're new in town and are taking trips into the jungle."

"On your feet," Barkow said.

"Where're we going?"

"We're going to have a little chat with Gary Appelton."

"No! I'll not take you there."

"Yes, you will or I'll take you across my knee and give you a spanking. You have five seconds to decide. 4… 3… 2…"

"Okay. I'll take you."

"Good choice." He muttered. "Lead the way."

They walked several blocks and came to a four storied building. The arched entrance was placed a few steps above the ground level sidewalk. Large double doors with brass door handles gleamed in the single hanging light above. There was nothing to indicate it was a hotel.

She led the way up the entrance stairs and pulled open the right hand door. "He's on the second floor," she said as she started up the stairs. Barkow followed. At the top of the stairway a wall-mounted fixture gave dim, yellow light to the hall. She opened the second door on the right and walked in as she called out, "I'm back Gary. I've brought company."

"Who the hell is this?"

"This is the man we've been following."

"Why did you bring him here, for Christ's sake?"

"Because he wants to talk to you."

"Well, I don't want to talk to him, so take him someplace else."

Barkow looked at Gary. He was somewhere in his thirties and was wearing a tee shirt and undershorts. His face showed a week's growth of beard. He had a pale complexion, dark hair, medium build and was barefoot. A scowl seemed to be his permanent facial expression.

"Listen, Appleton," Barkow said. "I have a few questions then I'll be on my way."

"Roni!" Appleton screamed. "Get this asshole out of our room before...." His voice ended abruptly in a gargle-sound as Barkow had him in a choke hold from behind. He had moved so fast Gary Appleton was not aware of how it happened. Barkow spoke in a low growl directly into Appleton's ear.

"I don't have time to waste on a stupid bastard like you. You can either answer my questions or you'll be dead in the next three minutes. He ground a knuckle into Appleton's scull behind his earlobe. The man squealed in pain.

"Who do you work for?"

"*International Times*," came the garbled answer.

"Why are you in Belize?"

"Story assignment." Again the knuckle brought amazing results.

"I was sent here to uncover the reason a huge drug cartel is taking over from local crime leaders."

"What Cartel?"

"Cortes"

"What've you found out?"

"I've got Roni canvassing suspects."

"What else?"

"That's it. We only been here a little over a week."

"Over a week and you have her following strangers around?"

"It was her idea. She's learning the tricks of being an international reporter."

"What the hell do you do?"

"I'm the lead reporter, the idea man."

Barkow threw Appleton across the room where he slammed into a wall and crumpled on the floor. "Lead reporter my ass. You don't lead and you have no ideas. Get dressed and get the hell out of here."

"This is our room and…." He turned his head and cowered as Barkow started toward him. "I'm going." He said and began crabbing away."

"Don't you dare hurt Gary?" Roni spoke up.

"Why not? What's this dirt-bag to you?"

"He's teaching me to be a world-wide reporter."

"He couldn't teach you to boil water. The quicker you get him out of your life, the better." Barkow snarled. "Whose idea was it to follow me around?"

"That was my idea," she spat.

"And you hired the bush hat guy. Why?"

"Because I have to study my books for the test."

"What test?"

"My reporter test. Gary was going to give it to me tonight."

"Yeah. I'll bet he was." Barkow said with disgust.

Gary came out wearing pants. "Shoes." Barkow barked.

He at once put on a pair of sandals

"Out!"

"Where can I go in the middle of the night" Gary whined.

"You, Appleton, can go to hell and don't come within my sight again." Barkow growled as Appleton slithered out the door.

Barkow turned to Roni with a broad smile and a twinkle in his eye. "I could hardly keep from laughing at that little pipsqueak."

"What will he do," She asked.

"Nothing. Probably hide in the bushes until I leave. I know his kind and you'd be better off without him."

"I know, Gary is not very professional, but I need him. He has some sort of hold on our boss and gets the plush assignments. When I get the title of International Reporter and a few good stories for the paper, I won't need Gary anymore and can move on with my career to another job. Until then I have to act like he's the greatest thing since sliced bread."

"What's this thing about a test?"

"Probably a ruse to get me in bed with him, but it ain't gonna happen," she said with a smile.

"Okay, kid. I got it. What would happen if you just dumped him and did the story on your own?"

"I can't. Not until he tells the editor I should be given full status as an overseas reporter, than I can act."

"Alright." Barkow said. "Play it your way. Do not follow me around because you will just get yourself hurt or more than likely killed. Poke around town and see if you can pick up any leads on this Cortes syndicate. Don't do anything foolish. Don't use Hector anymore. He'll cause more harm than good. Find out everything Appleton knows about this assignment."

"And what will you be doing," Roni said.

"I've a good lead going for my own reasons of being here. I think it will all tie in with what is happening in this country."

Barkow brought forth a blank business card, scribbled his sat-phone number and handed it to her. "Keep me informed on what you find out and I'll keep you tuned in on what I dig up."

"Sounds good, but Gary controls all the money. I can't do a whole lot on my own.

Barkow removed 600 dollars from his wallet and handed it to her.

"You're now on my payroll. Don't let Appleton know you have any money. Keep him out of the loop. I will soon be going back to the jungle, so I may not be around for a few days."

"How can I keep from telling Gary what I find out?"

"Who sends the stories in to the paper?"

"Gary does."

"Then it's up to you to take over that job. Once you're the one sending in the stories, you'll have control and can feed Gary whatever kind of line you want. Anything to keep him out of the way until you break the big one."

"It certainly sounds like a plan. We work together on getting the information of what is happening in this country and when the time comes I'll cover the news angle and you will complete whatever it is you are here for."

"I'm chasing down the whereabouts of a missing Lancair IV-P that was last seen here in Belize. I know when and where it landed in the jungle and have a lead on where they took it. Somehow I think it's all tied in with the crime wave taking place in the major cities of Belize."

While Barkow was talking to her, he realized she was more mature then he'd thought at first. Roni possessed a well curved figure with narrow waist, flared hips and shapely legs. Her breasts were neither large nor small. Barkow guessed her age to be in the mid to late twenties. She had a small mouth which made her brown eyes look larger than they actually were. Her dark brown hair was cut short in back, lengthening into waves on top with bangs swiping across her forehead.

"It sounds interesting," she replied.

CHAPTER TEN

BARKOW AWOKE IN his hotel room after three hours of sleep. He showered, shaved, dressed and went down to the hotel restaurant for breakfast. Drinking coffee and waiting for his food he took out the portable GPS and checked the flashing green dot for the canoes whereabouts. The lat/long position showed it still in the jungles of the Cockscomb Basin but further west then from where it started and still on the move.

Back in his room, the sat phone rang. Expecting it to be Laura he answered.

"Barkow."

"Hi Barkow, it's me, Roni."

"Hi Roni. What's up?"

"Gary never came back last night. Maybe he thinks you're still here."

"Do you have any idea where he would go?"

"Not really. He usually stayed here as far as I know. His cell phone, money and credit cards are still in his room."

"That don't sound good. I thought you and he were rooming together. This may be your chance to send something in to San Fran."

"What do you mean, rooming together?"

"Well, the guy was in his shorts and a tee shirt when we arrived."

"Oh no. We each have our separate bedrooms and were in the connected living room when we met him last night."

"Okay. Write up some sort of progress report today. If Gary doesn't come back, call your paper this evening and ask if they've heard from him. If not, tell them something big is going down and that Gary has disappeared so you thought you should tell them you have things covered; then give them your report."

"You mean report a fake story to the newspaper?"

"No, not at all. I mean send them a progress report on whatever information you have. Like a mysterious man arrived and is making helicopter trips into the jungle. He's been seen around Belize City asking questions. A woman he spoke to recently was found with her throat cut at the airport. That you are discreetly shadowing him and think you are on to something and you will continue to send in reports until Gary returns. Make it sound like you know more than you do."

"Oh! Then it's okay if I use you in the story?"

"Of course, but don't tell anything other than the truth and above all, Roni, do *not* tell them we are working together. You see, this is just a delaying tactic until you get something juicy but it will begin to put you in position to take over.

Another thing, I want you to be very cautious and aware of what is going on around you. The lid could come off this town at any moment. If you notice anyone is following you, go straight to the police station. Don't go into deserted streets after dark."

"I understand. Tell me, Barkow, you didn't have anything to do with Gary's disappearance, did you?"

"No, Roni, I didn't. I figured he would come back as soon as I left. Let's touch base tonight. How about dinner at my hotel, unless you have a better restaurant in mind?"

"The Radisson is as good as any in this town. How about seven for a time?"

"That's good. I'll meet you in the lobby tonight at seven."

"Bye, Barkow."

"Bye, Roni, take care."

Barkow sat for a moment staring into space and holding the phone, then called Laura at his condo, knowing she wouldn't have gone to work at the Blue Note yet. She answered on the second ring.

"Hello, Barkow. Is everything alright?"

"Everything's fine Laura, How're you doing?"

"Other than missing you, I'm doing fine."

"Yeah, I know what you mean. Are things running smooth at the Blue Note?"

"Like it was Teflon coated. I had a midnight supper with Bobby and Terry last night. They said to say 'hi' the next time you called. Bobby thinks we're building a solid clientele because he sees a lot of the same people coming in or a regular basis and has had to increase his drink order from the supplier."

"That's great. I know Bobby has a good sense of business."

"When you coming home?"

"Soon as I wrap this thing up. It's coming to a head as far as finding the plane. When I nail down the exact location where it's at, my end of the job's over."

"I can send you a hammer and a few nails if that will get you home faster."

"I'll be home soon." He smiled. "We can go out for dinner and dancing."

"Oh, Barkow. That sounds so good. Please hurry home. I'll be waiting."

"Okay, Laura. Have a great day and I'll see you soon.

"You too. Bye."

Barkow hung up and leaned back in his chair, letting his mind wander. *It was good to hear Laura's voice. When I talk with her I always become anxious to get back to Phoenix and be with her again. I find myself thinking of that girl a lot since I came on this trip. I won't tell her this place is a powder keg about to blow up. No point in making her worry. What could have happened to Appleton? I thought that little weasel would have gone back to the room as soon as I'd left. Roni seems like a good person. Maybe a bit gullible but a nice person. I'm glad she's not shacking up with Appleton and I hope she don't end up like Rosita. I should have cautioned her more than I did....*

He picked up the phone and called Hombre Blanco, undercover alias of the Phoenix Police who led the Gang Squad Department.

"Blanco," answered a raspy voice.

"Hey Blanco, Barkow here. How're you doing?"

"Doing real good. Heard you were out of the country."

"Yeah, I'm in Belize tracking down a lost plane."

"What can I do for you?"

"The lid is about to blow off this country. You heard anything about a major drug deal going down in Central America?"

"Lots of rumbling about someone setting up a new operation, but I don't know where or who."

"You've heard of the Cortes Syndicate?"

"Who hasn't?"

"That's the outfit moving into Belize. It must have something to do with my missing Lancair because I keep running into that name."

"Treat them with kid gloves, my friend. They've offed more guys then I can count. What are they doing?"

"Just a lot of strong-arm stuff and there haves been some murders and missing people. They're also flooding the market with cheap drugs."

"Listen, Barkow. I can get you the official book on them if you want. It may give you an insight on what they are up to."

"Thanks Blanco. I'm working with a reporter from The San Francisco International Times Newspaper. Her name is Veronica Lowen and goes by the name of Roni. She's working with a reporter named Gary Appleton, who is now missing. Can you get her email address and send the book to her laptop. I'll tip her off its coming and to be kept top secret."

"I should be able to do that. I take it you don't want the newspaper to know what I'm sending. Right?"

"That's right Blanco. Keep this little favor under wraps. I appreciate it and I'll tip you off if anything comes up that concerns drugs or gangs in Arizona."

Good Deal, glad I can help. Your old friend Juan is keeping mum about anything he had to do with you or yours. You must have put the fear of God in him."

"Maybe more than that." Barkow chuckled. "Thanks for your help, I'll buy you a drink when I get home."

Barkow spent the day searching the Spanish influenced colonial architecture and the never-ending events of music and festivals for any clues that could help him find out what was going on beneath the current of everyday life in Belize. He engaged in conversations with a broad spectrum of people, from waiters and store clerks to taxi drivers and patrons of bars. The basic result was that most locals knew something bad was taking place in Belize, although none offered any clue as to what it was. An old Mayan woman on a park bench told him of three men who had mysteriously gone missing, over the past two weeks, when they were working in the jungle. Three unconnected white men, on three different jobs, that took them to different places in the outlying countryside, never returned to their families.

That evening, Barkow met Roni in the hotel lobby at seven. She was wearing a colorful Mexican skirt, a peasant blouse and carrying a backpack by its straps. He smiled and led her into the restaurant. He had arranged for a table in the corner of the room that had a view of the entire seating area and the entrance door to the restaurant.

"We can sit here, Roni," he said. "I hope you know, that you're in grave danger now." He said. "You need to realize what this Cortes Syndicate is capable of. Murder, rape, riot, torture and kidnapping is a way of life for them. How did things go today?"

"Very productive. I found some more news that happened here and called the San Fran newspaper with an upgrade on my story information."

"That's great. Have they heard from Appleton?"

"Nope. They thought it was strange that he has disappeared. Like you said, they seemed delighted that I was on top of things and told me to keep up the good work and to keep them informed."

"What sort of stuff did you give them?"

"Exactly the way you told me to put it, plus I have a couple of new facts. I was talking with a Bureau of Mayan Affairs Inspector today. He informed me of a shadow group of Maya who live in the jungles and shun civilization. They call themselves '*The Jaguars*' and are trying to follow an ancient religion of some sort. The Bureau is trying to infiltrate them but has not succeeded so far."

"That's odd. I wonder if somehow the Jaguar group has anything to do with my missing Lancair?"

"Could be. By the way, a note was slipped under my door while I was out, saying I should not give any information to my paper."

"That's not good. They know you're working for a newspaper. You really have to watch yourself now. I don't like the fact you live in that building out of the mainstream of traffic. Why're you there anyway?"

"It's an apartment set up by the newspaper. They lease it from the owners of the building I think."

"I don't like it. I want you out of that place and into a decent hotel."

"It will be okay, Barkow. It seems safe to me."

"No. It's not safe. It's too far away from everything and they know you're there plus you've already been warned. When did you get the note?"

"Sometime during the day."

"When and how did you give the information to the paper?"

"Around five by phone."

"Cell or room phone?"

"Room."

A waitress came to their table and took their order. After she left, Barkow said, "They've got your room bugged. Probably rigged with a camera too. What's in that room that is of prime importance to your mission here?"

She thought a moment, then said, "Actually nothing except my clothes and bathroom stuff. I have my backpack with me. My laptop, purse, camera and phone are in it because I thought you may want to see all the notes I have taken since I started looking into the situation."

"That's good. How did you get to this hotel tonight?"

"I came by cab."

"Do you have a car here?"

"No. We had a rented car but I guess Gary has it."

"Alright. That's all good," he smiled. Here comes our food. Let's eat."

While eating, they carried on some small-talk of little consequence. *She seems to be oblivious to the fact she may be in grave danger. I'm surprised they even gave her a note.* Barkow thought. *Maybe they want to keep tabs on what she finds out and maybe that place she's in is a death trap.*

They finished eating and enjoyed an after-dinner drink.

"I will be leaving for another excursion into the jungle tomorrow or the next day." Barkow said. "It all depends on some information I am waiting to receive."

"Something to do with that plane, I suppose."

"Yes. As soon as we are finished here, you are going to get a room at this hotel. I don't want you to go back to the apartment."

"Oh, Barkow, don't be silly. There's no good reason to pay for another room when the paper has provided a nice apartment."

"Listen, Roni. Your very life is in great danger. You have no idea what this Cortes Syndicate is capable of. You are getting a room here and that's final. I had them checked out and they are in control of 78% of the drug traffic in all of Central America. Something big is happening in Belize and it concerns Cortes."

"This may be the story of a lifetime," Roni said.

"Yeah, it may be. I have a friend emailing you the crime book on the Cortes Syndicate. It will help you flesh out your story on them. I'm doing this on the sly so don't tell anyone you have it. Destroy the damn thing and everything in it when this job is finished. Understand?"

"I got it. Thanks Barkow. With all the crime going on, it

may be a good idea to leave the apartment, but what will I tell the paper?"

"Tell them nothing except for the stories you call in. If they ask, be evasive."

He watched her as she considered his remark. Two tiny lines of concern appeared between her eyes. She was absently staring at her coffee cup when suddenly she flicked her attention to him in a quick glance, then back to her cup without moving any part of her anatomy except her eyelids.

"Tell me something," she said. "Is there an ulterior motive for my staying in your hotel tonight?"

Barkow smiled. "Do you think I'll come creeping to your room during the night? You are a beautiful woman, but no, I don't have romantic intentions. You can go by yourself and register for a room and tell them your hotel information is to be kept in strict confidence. I'm helping you because I see the benefit to both for information shared between us.

"Thanks, Barkow. I thought it would be wise to get that little matter settled."

"It's not a problem, Roni, but I want to impress on you how volatile the situation is. In fact, I don't want you out of this hotel after dark unless you clear it with me. I'm not trying to run your life, my intent is to keep you alive."

"You certainly seem to know what you're doing and I think you can be trusted."

"I know exactly what I'm doing, and yes Roni, you can trust me."

"I do trust you, Barkow. If we are to be working together for a while I think it is important we know each other's room number, so we can make inter-room phone calls and be able to go to each other's room if necessary."

"I agree, but was hesitant to bring it up because you would have thought I was setting you up for a score.

"Yes," she smiled, "I would have."

"You should request a room on the second floor, the same as mine. I can keep better tabs on you that way."

"Alright. I will go check in and give you a call to your room when I get mine."

"My room is 212. Call me when you're settled."

"Will do," she said as she gathered up her gear and left the restaurant.

Barkow signed for the meal and returned to his room. A half hour later the room phone rang.

"Barkow."

"Roni here. I'm in room 222 just down the hall and around the corner from you."

"Thanks for calling. Today or tomorrow I'll leave for the jungle again. You should check in with the Belize Police Department tomorrow. Here, it's not like the States, where each city has its own police, but more like a country wide army of sorts. They are the law enforcement branch of the government. See if you can set up an inside contact with them and find out what they know about what's going down. Don't go back to your apartment and don't stay out past sunset."

"What do you mean by an inside contact?"

"I mean, try to find someone, anyone, who you can contact by phone in order to give or get information. You need a pipeline into their ranks so you can know what is happening that doesn't make the papers."

"Oh! You want me to get a snitch?"

"Not really. More like get a friend who you can chat with about what happens in the Police Department?"

"Okay, I'll give it a try."

"It's time you learned how to be a newspaper reporter. They all do it, you know."

"Alright. You want to meet for dinner tomorrow?"

"Yes, if I'm still in town. Same time, same place."

"See you then. Bye."

"Bye, Roni."

CHAPTER ELEVEN

THE NEXT MORNING, Barkow checked the GPS. The green, blinking signal had stopped.

It means they've either reached their destination or have stopped for some other reason. I'll give them some time and if they're not on the move again, I'll go and hunt 'em down.

He drove to Tourism Village, parked and walked to *Vito's Express Flights*. At the counter was a young woman wearing a basic green circle skirt which could be casual or dressy. A sleeveless white top with a Mayan flower print and sandals. She was in the process of pinning a poster of a swooping helicopter on the wall behind the counter.

"Good morning," he said.

"Good morning, sir," she said as she pressed in the final pushpin.

When she turned around, Barkow was struck by her Italian beauty. It was obvious she had the ability to put together an ensemble of clothes and look very attractive wearing them. She came around the counter and crossed the room with a certain confidence that in itself was very striking. He suddenly had the impression that she was in-general, more emotional than most women.

Whether welling up in tears listening to Julio Iglesias or rapturously throwing her arms around me for no good reason. There would never be a dull moment with this woman.

"What may I help you with?" She said in a friendly and business-like manner.

"I stopped by to see Vito."

"My father will be here," she looked at her watch, "in about twenty minutes."

"May I wait here for him or would you prefer I return later?"

"You may wait here." She gave him a dazzling smile. "Are you the customer, father is flying in and out of the jungle?"

"Yes. My name is Barkow."

"My name is Lolita Vito. Everyone calls me Lola."

His smile, the one which woman could not resist, flashed. "My name is George Bennett Barkow. I prefer to be called Barkow."

Why he told her his full name was a mystery because he never offered those given names to anyone else. She had the effect of making him feel as though he had known her for years.

This woman would want chivalry in a relationship. Little things like getting up to give her your seat if none were available. She would like the door to be held open for her. Small courtesies, like pulling the chair out for her in a restaurant or opening the car door for her would be anticipated.

"Of course, Barkow." Her melodious voice broke his chain of thoughts. "I am pleased to make your acquaintance."

"And I am pleased to meet the lovely Lolita Vito, known as Lola." He said.

The door opened and Vito entered.

"I see you have met my beautiful daughter." His voice boomed.

"I have indeed. Her beauty is surpassed only by the musical charm of her voice. She obviously takes after her mother," Barkow said with a grin.

"Thank you my friend." Vito acknowledged the compliment. "What brings you to my door?"

"It appears the canoe I'm following has stopped. Is your service available to take Con and me on a flight at sunrise tomorrow?"

"It is and will be ready at dawn."

"Thank you Vito. If there is any change in plans I'll call you this evening. It was my pleasure to meet you, Lola."

"The pleasure is mine, Barkow. I wish you well."

Barkow nodded to both, walked out of the shop and back to his car. On a hunch he drove to the park where he had first met Roni. He drove slowly past the park on the street to the building where she and Appleton were staying and stared at the difference in appearance. A section of the brick building's second story lay in rubble at its base. He drove the car a block past and parked by a row of palm trees. Walking back he saw a man standing at the side of the semi-demolished structure.

"This is not a safe place to be passing the time, Hector." Barkow said as he approached.

"I came looking for Roni. How could this have happened?"

"Someone rigged it with explosives and blew it apart. That's how."

"I'm afraid to go look and see if Roni is in the wreckage."

"Wait here, I'll take a look." Barkow said and went to the front door of the building. Inside, he climbed the stairway and found the first several feet of hallway on the second story still existed. A single glance showed the apartment of Roni and Appleton had been totally destroyed. He went downstairs and to the damaged side of the building. A methodical search through the debris convinced him no human remains were there. He returned to Hector.

"There are no bodies in the wreckage of the apartment."

"Thank God," Hector said.

A man came from across the street and walked over to where the two men stood.

"When did the explosion happen?" Barkow asked the newcomer.

"About three in the morning."

"Was anyone injured or killed?"

"No, by the favor of God, no one was hurt." He crossed himself.

"Thanks." Barkow said as he turned to Hector. "When did you see Roni last?"

"Two days ago."

"Okay. Go home, Hector, and do not get any more involved in what's going down. Things are very dangerous now. Roni had dinner with me last night and I convinced her to stay at the same hotel so she was alright this morning."

"I've been looking for her all day and calling her cell but never received an answer." Hector said in a worried voice.

"She's supposed to meet for dinner again tonight in the hotel. I'll tell her to call you so you won't worry."

"Thanks, Barkow," Hector said and the two men went their separate ways.

When Barkow returned to the Radisson, he made a call to Laura and chatted with her for a while but remained silent about the dangerous turn of events in Belize.

Later, in the restaurant, he waited for the reporter to show up at seven. He ordered a drink and began to brood.

I should never have let Roni go out on her own. I knew things were dangerous and getting worse. They blew up her apartment in the middle of the night so I was right on track to keep her at the hotel. Now she's not here and it feels as though it's my fault. She knows my satellite number and can call if she's in trouble…if she's able to call.

Barkow tried calling her cell. It connected but went straight to voicemail. He waited in the restaurant, drinking bourbon on the rocks, until eight o'clock, a full hour past the agreed on time to meet.

The ironclad-certainty arrived like a roll of thunder. *She'd call if she was going to be late. Roni is either dead or has been kidnapped, just like Appleton.*

Barkow returned to his room and began going through his gear for the helicopter trip the next morning when the phone rang, he quickly picked up.

"Barkow."

"Hello, Mr. Barkow. This is the Belize Police Department calling. May I speak with Veronica Lowen?"

"Miss Lowen is not here."

"My name is Officer Michael Taber. Can you tell me when she will return?"

"I cannot. We were supposed to meet for dinner at seven. She never arrived."

"She told me to call you if I could not reach her on the cell phone."

"She was obviously in trouble. When did you see her last?"

"She stopped me on the street today just before lunch. She seemed out of breath and wanted me to walk with her for a ways. I think someone was following her. She gave me her number and yours also, then asked me to please call her this evening and if she could not be reached, to call you."

"What else did you talk about?"

"Actually, nothing. When I began to question her she said, 'this is my stop, I'll see you later' then stepped into a crowded store and disappeared. She was plainly ditching me."

"She's a reporter for a San Francisco newspaper. Maybe she's onto a story."

"I thought it could be something of the sort. She seemed to want information although she never came right out and asked for it. There's so much crime happening in Belize, I'm now suspicious of everyone. There was an attempt to kidnap a young woman today in broad daylight."

"Yeah, I know what you mean. I work for Great Metro Insurance and I'm trying to locate a missing Lancair, last traced to this location."

"Have you had any luck?"

"I found the jungle site where it landed, was stripped then taken away. I think I have a lead on where it is and will know more after tomorrow."

"Thank you for your time, Mr. Barkow. Please ask her to call me, if you see Miss Lowen again."

"Will do. Have a good evening," Barkow said and hung up. The phone rang almost at once.

"Barkow."

"Hello, Barkow. It's me, Hector. Did you and Roni have dinner tonight?"

"Hello, Hector. No, she never showed up."

"I'm worried sick about her, Barkow. I think I'll go check out some of the places where she may be and just lost track of time."

"Listen to me, Hector." Barkow said. "Do not leave your home. You may be in danger as well as Roni. Were you two following anyone other than me?"

"No. Lately it was only you."

"Alright. Now is the time, Hector, for you to be real smart. Do not go out at night and always stay on the busy streets during the day. Something very bad is happening. I'll be gone for a day or two and will call you when I get back in town. Under no circumstances are you to delve into any crime matters, for they are way above your pay-grade and it would only get you killed. If you have any information regarding Roni or Appleton, or if you fear you are in danger for any reason, I want you to call Officer Michael Taber of the Belize Police. Tell him I gave you his name.

"Okay, Barkow. Thanks for the contact at the police department. I'll sit tight. Good luck and call me when you get back."

"Bye, Hector." Barkow hung up and immediately the phone rang again.

"Barkow," he answered.

"Barkow, this is Vito. I have been trying to reach you. Two men came into the office this afternoon and tried to abduct Lola."

"Were you there?"

"No. I was at the shop preparing the bird for tomorrow."

"You said they tried to get Lola. What happened?"

"Two men, she said they were big and looked like White/Mexican half-breeds, came into the office and while one stood by the door watching the street, the other said something like, 'she was coming with them and maybe he'd marry her. He also said she looked as though she could give up many little Jaguars.

"Damn it," Barkow swore. "I think they've snatched the reporter, Veronica, and have now tried to get your daughter."

"I'm not sure, Barkow, but Lola was having none of it and

pulled her 410 from under the counter. He started for her and she put a load of buckshot into his side."

"Good for her. Then what happened?"

"She said the guy started screaming and hobbled for the door dripping blood all over. He turned and said, 'I'll be back for you, bitch.' Then they ran out of there and she called the police."

"They definitely planned to grab her. Thank God she had a weapon."

"I know and I'm sending Lola and her mother to stay with my brother in Jamaica until this crazy crime wave blows over in Belize."

"I'm glad she's safe at home, Vito. Those reporters I've been working with are also missing and last night their apartment was destroyed by a bomb. Are you ready to go tomorrow?"

"Yes, I'm ready but we need to put departure off until eight. I will be putting my wife and daughter on a plane for Jamaica at seven fifteen. The quicker they are out of Belize the better. I also know of two young women and three men who have mysteriously gone missing lately. I do not like it, Barkow. Not at all."

"I don't like it either, Vito. I've heard of those same people. By the way, do you know a Police officer named Michael Taber?"

"I know Mike. He is a good man. He and Lola are friends.

"I haven't met him face to face, but he seemed like a good person. I'll meet you at eight. Tell Lola I'm happy she wasn't harmed."

"I will, Barkow. See you in the morning,"

Barkow hung up and at once called the number for Con.

"Hello." The familiar female voice answered.

"Hello. Is the jungle man there?"

"He is not available. Is this Barkow?"

"Yes, can you give Con a message for me?"

"Certainly."

"Please tell him our departure is at eight o'clock tomorrow instead of sunrise."

"I'll see he has the message. Thank you for calling, Mr. Barkow."

"You're welcome. Good night." Barkow said and hung up.

This situation is coming to a head and may explode any moment. Roni is gone, either captured or dead. Now they've tried to get Lola and I heard of three guys from England missing from different jobs while working in the jungle. For some reason it seems like they want Caucasians. What would be the purpose behind that? There are no ransom notes which I know of. Maybe it's something to do with the slave trade. If they have Roni did they get her laptop and find the crime book on the Cortes syndicate?

Barkow suddenly stood up and left his room. He strode down the hall and around the corner to room 222. He placed his room keycard in the slot, which would not open the lock but it would hold a certain pin inside the mechanism in an open position. From a leather case on his belt he removed a Swiss Army Knife. It had a wide assortment of different tools. He at once began disassembling the card lock on Roni's room door. In a matter of minutes he had it apart and the door open. A quick check showed the only thing missing was her purse. The laptop lay on a small table. He scooped it up and went back to the hall where he reassembled the card lock, removed his keycard and went back to his room. Searching the laptop gave no further information. It was pass-code protected and he had no way of getting into the files.

CHAPTER TWELVE

BARKOW RECALLED WHAT he had learned about the remote jungle tribe. Descendants of the ancient Maya civilization, now gone for thousands of years, still live in their old domains, although most have modernized as did the rest of the world. In Belize, a small group of those descendants had recently split from the modern world and chose to live in the uninhabited areas of the country, calling themselves *The Jaguars*. The leaders of this group were made up of disgruntled individuals who not only had the desire to live as did their ancestors of long ago, but longed to bring back some of the old customs. They lived deep in the swamps and jungles of Belize and traveled game trails and uncharted rivers.

Barkow did not know the jaguar was the god of the underworld in ancient Mayan mythology, symbolic of darkness and the night sun. It ruled over the celestial forces of day and night, and was seen as a representation of leadership, control and confidence. Ancient Mayans revered the jaguar and accorded it immense religious importance, second only to the serpent.

Six years prior to Barkow's arrival in Belize, an Aztec Indian, named Coatl' entered Belize with a large bounty for his capture due to his deep involvement in the Mexican drug wars. He was on the run from the Mexican Army and crossed the border between Mexico and Belize to lose himself in the jungle swamps of the Cockscomb Basin. In time, Coatl' crossed trails with a small band of hunters who told him of a tribe of Indians who lived at the end of a river and shunned the modern world.

It would be the ideal place to hide out for a while, Coatl' thought.

It took over two years of searching unexplored rivers until he found one ending in a whirlpool at the base of a huge, jungle covered, granite upheaval. He was unaware at the time of discovery, how fortunate it was his given name had been taken from the Nahuatl language which had been spoken by ancient Aztecs, as well as did the Mayans long before them. Those Aztecs of old had worshiped one of the main Mesoamerican deities called Huitzilopochtli, who was represented as a feathered serpent. The name means *"beautiful serpent"* (In Nahuatl, 'Quetzalli' means beautiful and 'coatl' means snake.)

⊙ BARKOW AND CON reached Vito's Scenic Flights at 7:45 on a bright, sunny morning. Vito arrived a few minutes later.

"Hi, Vito," Barkow greeted him. "Did you get your family on a flight out of Belize?"

"Yes, thank God. They are safely away from this crime ridden country."

"It'll take a lot of worry off your mind. Do you have any idea who the two men, which attacked your daughter, worked for?"

"No, but the Police suspect they are tied into the drug trafficking in Belize. It seems they've been in a few bar fights the past couple of weeks. Lola gave the authorities a good sketch of her assailants."

"I'm glad she's safe now. Do you think she was targeted because of you giving me flights to the jungle?"

"It could be the reason. If they come smelling around me I'll do more then give them buckshot."

"If I'm around, you can always call on me for help if you need it."

"Thanks Barkow. The bird is ready for take-off," Vito said. "Let's get aboard."

The helicopter lifted gracefully away from its pad and veered away on a course to the lat/long position reported by the signal sender on the dugout's hull. As they approached the exact location the signal appeared to emanate from the base of a jungle covered ridge. There was no place in the thickly forested area where Vito could land the copter. He began flying a search-circle and found a small clear spot approximately two miles up the slope of the ridge. It was not level and the reason for a lack of vegetation was due to it being a mammoth, granite boulder protruding from the earth. Vines and creepers clung to the sides of the great rock a short distance above the huge jungle trees growing directly to its boundaries.

Vito's voice crackled over the headphones. "I can set you down on the rock but cannot actually land because it is too great a slope. You would have to jump from the struts to the surface from about three or four feet, while I hover. Do you want to keep looking for a better place?"

"No," Barkow answered. "This is alright. We will jump from the ship."

"Don't forget. The rotor blades will be spinning above you, creating a strong downdraft. As soon as you are on the rock, lay down and I'll lift away quickly."

Barkow looked at Con. The guide nodded and gave a thumbs up. "Okay Vito we got it. Con will go first and I'll give you a pat on the shoulder just before I jump. Give me five seconds and lift away."

The body of the helicopter hovered above the proposed landing site. It slowly began to drop downward, closer and closer to the rock which proved to be on a steeper slope then what it looked like in the air. Con slid the door on his side open and sat sideways on the seat, putting his feet on the landing strut. When the strut was within three feet of the rock the opposite strut was six or eight feet from the downward sloping surface. Con jumped. Barkow slipped into his seat, put his feet on the strut, reached over to give the pilot a slap on the shoulder and jumped for the surface with legs spread apart so not to roll when he landed. In the roaring downdraft he could hear nothing but suddenly it was gone and the whap-whap-whap of the copter blades could be heard fading away.

They lay spread-eagled, face down on the rock. Vito circled

them one time from a distance, blinked his landing lights twice then locked on a course for home. On the sun-drenched granite surface, the squawking and chirping of jungle birds could be heard far below.

Both gingerly rose to a kneeling position on the grainy surface of the massive boulder, facing uphill. They looked at each other and smiled at the absurd situation they were in. The colossal rock was rounded on top with no level space, much like the large end of a boiled egg. All sides had a downward slope changing into a steep grade quickly becoming a sheer drop.

"How are we going to get down?" Barkow said.

"Boss man wait. Con find way down." He at once began to do a sort of sideway crawl while all the time facing uphill, knowing a single slip could cause a downward slide to death. The rounded crown of the rock was perhaps thirty feet in diameter and topped out some twenty feet above Barkow's head. Con was soon out of sight beyond the boulder's curvature.

Glancing over his shoulder, Barkow could not see where jungle trees came against the side of the rock. He was afraid to move farther downward on the slope because it became too steep and he would surely fall to his demise. The drop could easily be eighty to a hundred feet straight down. After waiting for perhaps thirty minutes, Con came into sight from the opposite side of the surface from where he started.

"What did you find?"

"Find vine."

"How big?"

"Big as finger."

"Which one?"

"Little finger."

"Can we use it to climb down?"

The little guide solemnly shook his head. "Vine go sideways on rock."

"Nothing else?"

Con shook his head.

"I want to see the vine. It has to come from somewhere."

"Follow Con." He began crabbing sideways back in the direction from which he'd come, always facing uphill. Barkow followed. After moving sideways for about fifteen minutes, Con stopped.

"Look down, see vine."

Barkow looked and sure enough, about two yards below his feet was a vine, of half-inch diameter, stretching across the face of the rock. Along the outside edges grew tiny, thread-like tentacles reaching out to curl around any slight distortion in the granite surface. The vine came upward from below and curved horizontally across some fifteen feet of the boulder face, then turned downward to lose itself below the curvature of the rock.

"Okay, Con, I got it figured. Get close to me and open my backpack."

He moved over to Barkow who lay face down, spread eagled on the rounded surface and unsnapped the flap of the pack strapped to Barkow's back.

"There's a zipper along the edge of the pack on my right side. Open it and bring out the white nylon cord, machine-coiled into a ten inch roll."

In a moment Con said, "Here cord."

Barkow managed to take the cord with one hand and with his teeth pull the bitter end of it from the coiled roll. He carefully transferred the end to Con.

"Here's what you do, Con. I weigh 230 pounds so I'll remain spread-eagled on this rock and you need to, very slowly, climb headfirst down my leg until you can reach the vine. Holding onto my leg one-handed, with your other hand, you'll have to slip the end of this cord under the vine the pull it back to you and climb back up my body, bringing the cord with you. Got it?"

"Con can do." He said.

The guide replaced the coil of cord in the pocket and closed the zipper to all but a small opening than replaced the flap on Barkow's backpack. He made certain the cord pulled freely from the pack. Taking the end of the cord in his mouth, slowly turned his body around as Barkow adjusted both arms and legs out wide, hugging the face of the rock as best he could. Con, very slowly stretched out alongside Barkow and started inching toward the vine. He hooked his leg around Barkow's foot.

Ever so slowly he inched downward while reaching with his hand now holding the end of the cord. Unhurriedly he stretched to the limit of his reach, then allowed himself to deliberately slip a tiny bit downwards, knowing a wrong calculation would send both him and Barkow sliding off the side of the rock to death below.

Con held the bitter-end of the cord between the second and third finger-tips. He touched the vine and with the dexterity of a magician lifted the creeper with his ring finger and slipped the bitter end of the cord under it. A slight twist of his wrist and he had the cord pinched between thumb and finger. He slowly brought the hand to his mouth and clinched his teeth on the cord, then began the unhurried process of working his way backwards, up Barkow's leg. The entire process took thirty-five minutes. Both men were drenched with sweat and gasping for breath when Con at last lay beside Barkow.

After they were breathing normally again, they started working upward, on hands and knees, toward the crown of the rock. On arrival, they rested, more or less in comfort, spread out across the rounded topmost knoll. Barkow asked Con to remove a coil of braided mountain-climbing rope from his backpack. He held the bitter end of the parachute cord which now went down the face of the rock, under the vine and back up to the coil of cord still in the zippered pocket. Con cut the cord near the pack and Barkow secured both ends together with double bowline knots, forming a completed circle. Beginning from where they were, the cord went down around the vine and back to them. Next he passed the end of the braided rope through the cord circle and pulled half of the hundred foot length through the loop. On one end he tied a hangman's knot with the noose-loop pulled up tight and the bitter end tucked through it hard against the coiled rope. It created a sort of handle on the rope's end. He then tossed both fifty foot lengths of braided rope over the side of the rock, letting them fall freely down the opposite side from where the cord went under the vine.

Barkow looked at Con and smiled. "What do you think of our escape off this rock," He asked.

Con solemnly nodded his head. "Is good." He muttered.

"The braided rope is only quarter-inch line but strong enough to hold both of us if necessary." Barkow said. "It would be difficult to hold onto one line but with the two doubled you should be able to marry the lines together and create enough material so you can go hand over hand down the side of the rock to the forest below, providing it's not over fifty feet to the bottom. If it's farther you'll have to yell up to me and I'll allow one side to shorten while you hold on to the other end."

"If vine no come loose, it work." Con said.

"I think the vine will hold from the way it grows up then over and down the side of the rock. If not we're both in for a long drop. I weigh twice as much as you, therefore you go first. When you are down, I'll follow."

"Barkow friend." Con said, gently nodding his head. "Friend go first."

"No. I'm heavier. If I break the vine, maybe Con would not."

"Con no want go first." The little guide said and turned his face away from Barkow.

"Don't be foolish Con. You will go first."

"Con no go first." The jungle man refused to turn his head and face Barkow.

Barkow was exasperated. "Con, you are my friend and I am your friend, but, I am also your boss man. Right?"

After thinking about it a minute, Con admitted in a quiet voice, "Barkow boss man," while he stared into space.

"Boss man say, Con go first."

"No. Con afraid go first."

"Yes, I say you go first. Con is not afraid, he's just obstinate."

"Bah! Barkow have hard head like rock." With his point

made, Con crawled over and straddled the two braided lines going down the face of the boulder.

"Remove your backpack first Con. It will take a little weight off." Barkow said.

"Sure, Barkow boss man." Con said as he stripped off his backpack.

"Does Con know how to marry two lines together?" Barkow said.

"Con know."

"Keep the lines married so they cannot slip. It makes them thicker, easier to grip and stronger. Yell at me if you run out of rope and then switch to the left one with the knotted end. You'll be able to hold onto the knot on the end of the rope. Okay?"

"Okay. Barkow good friend. Con go now."

"Have a safe trip down my friend." Barkow said.

Con married the two ropes together and pulled all the slack out then slowly stood up and leaned back. The lines went taunt but did not give. He started slowly taking small backward steps with first one hand holding the lines together then grasping farther down with the other doing the same.

"Goodbye friend Barkow." The words floated up as Con disappeared out of Barkow's line of sight.

"See you on the bottom, friend Con." Barkow called after him.

Barkow placed both hands loosely around the two braided ropes running from the loop of parachute cord, now taunt as a fiddle string.

If the bloody vine gives away, I'll hang on to these damned ropes as long as my strength holds out, he thought as the minutes crawled past.

Suddenly... all tension vanished... as both lengths of braided rope went slack.

CHAPTER THIRTEEN

IT HAD HAPPENED so quickly, Barkow's mind fled to the horrifying thought that Con had lost his grip and fallen to the jungle floor. "Con!" he called. "Con, are you alright?" He shouted in panic.

The voice of his friend floated up from below. "Con, okay."

Relief flooded through Barkow's body as the dread of losing his friend was lifted. He let out a sigh of relief and realized he had been holding his breath.

"Are you on the ground?" He shouted.

"Con on limb. Send down packs."

"Will do."

Barkow stripped off his pack, took out the roll of cord and tied the end to both backpacks. He rapidly paid out the cord lowering the backpacks until the line went limp. He tied the cord off on its own factory roll and let that also slide out of sight down the wall of rock. He straddled the double rope lines, married both together and picked them up. Barkow stood up slowly and leaned back letting his weight test the holding power of the vine. It seemed sturdy enough and he began his decent hand by hand, walking backward down the doubled length of rope. As he came down the sheer face of the rock he soon saw tree tops below him and heard Con's voice.

"Go under canopy, move left and come down." Con called.

Barkow lowered himself past the treetops into the shade below and began working over to his left. He felt Con grab his foot and guide it to a tree limb and was soon sitting on the branch of a huge breadfruit tree. The knot he'd tied on the end of the rope dangled a few yards below him.

"How far to the ground?" he said.

Con shook his head. "Too many leaves. I see backpacks go past."

Barkow reached over and gripped the guide's shoulder. "You are a good friend Con. At least we won't go hungry even if the fruit does taste like sawdust. The large thick leaves have a central stem with parts branching off and will bleed a milky juice, which is useful for boat caulking. Let's get down from this tree." With that said, he grasped the rope with the knotted end and hand over hand pulled the braided rope through the loop of parachute cord at the top of the rock. When he had the entire hundred foot length of rope coiled and over one shoulder, he secured the loops together beneath his opposite armpit. Limb by limb they made their way down the great tree. It was easily the largest breadfruit tree Barkow had ever saw but only half as tall as the huge kapoks of 200 feet. He estimated the breadfruit's height to be in excess of eighty feet.

Back on solid ground, the two friends gathered their backpacks and relaxed in the shade on the forest floor. Barkow lay full length using his pack for a pillow as he looked up the side of the gigantic boulder.

"Thank God, the jungle provided a vine growing along the face of the rock. If it had not been there we'd still be trying to figure out a way down." He said.

"Jungle my friend." Con said.

When fully rested from their ordeal, they strapped on backpacks and began making their way downhill through the flora, toward the location of the signal source. The shaded jungle floor was choked with lush, tropical vegetation. A wonderland of huge elephant-eared plants and eight foot tree-fern, with arcing wide, lacey fronds sweeping close to the ground. Leaf festooned vines, scattered with brilliant blooms, hung from tree limbs high above. As they approached a small tree with dark green leaves, wavy on leaf margins, hiding small red berries, Con suddenly spoke.

"No Boss man. No go near che chem tree. Go around," he said as he herded Barkow out and around the tree.

"What's the matter with it?" Barkow demanded.

"Che-chem posion tree. Make skin blister."

"You mean like poison oak or ivy?"

"Yes Boss. Che-chem very bad." Con said as he stared at Barkow and nodded his head slowly up and down. "Some people, no touch che-chem leaves or bark, yet get bad sores. Very bad." Barkow took careful note, not knowing it was called a Savanna White Poisonwood tree.

Overhead a boisterous flock of green parrots skittered through the trees and virtually disappeared when landing among the leaves on a tree limb, to feed on the fruit.

Making their way through a small stand of Logwood trees, used as a valuable dyewood, they surprised a small group of Peccary. The pig-like animals with thin legs and thick necks, were rooting in the soil for fruit, seeds, and small creatures; their strong musk odor permeated the air. With grunts and snorts they scattered away from the two men.

Swinging through the trees from limb to limb, a group of spider monkeys, with reddish fur, crossed above the two men making their way downhill. Barkow recalled reading how spider monkeys separate during the day into small groups of all-male and all-female, then go their different ways. They rejoin at night into one group and sleep together. Interesting because of all the primates, only spider monkeys, chimpanzees and humans have that trait.

They'd traveled approximately two miles past acacia, cypress and the showy buttonwood bushes, when the sloping terrain flattened out. The jungle guide in the lead stopped and held his hand up as he listened intently. Barkow watched as Con stood like a statue, his head bent slightly to one side. Suddenly the guide turned to Barkow and gave the sign for silence and motioned him to stay, then silently disappeared into the rainforest. Barkow knew if they got separated it would be difficult for him to find Con. The Mayan guide seemed to have no difficulty in knowing exactly where they were and could easily come and go as he pleased. Barkow knelt down on one knee to wait. Some twenty minutes later Con appeared and kneeled beside him.

"We close where river end," he said. "It go round and round." He swirled his hand in a slow, small circle. "Fall in jungle floor."

"How far?"

"Come. Con show."

They moved forward skirting rubber plants and bamboo thickets, through fern and broad-leafed plants, weaving between trees draped with hanging vines. Con stopped before a huge tree fern and lay upon the ground, motioning Barkow do the same. They wriggled forward beneath the sweeping fern fronds to the very edge of a sheer drop-off. Looking down, some 300 feet below, Barkow made out the swirling, green water of a whirlpool. It appeared to have a diameter close to twenty yards. They lay at the top of a massive granite upheaval, directly above the circular moving current, bordered by a myriad of fern, palms, bamboo growths and several tall kapok trees shrouded with large, climbing, Allamanda vines with showy, bright yellow flowers and shiny, green leaves. The scene was so beautiful it could have been a perfectly designed movie-set of a tropical paradise.

Barkow wriggled out of his backpack and brought out the GPS to find they were situated practically on top of the blinking green dot. Somewhere below them, beneath the trees was the dugout, with hull-attached signal sender. They moved back from the edge and worked their way downhill through thickly growing tropical plants and around to the opposite side of the whirlpool. If one could see the topography of the area without plant growth, it would appear to rise upwards from where the river created a whirlpool as it tried to enter a fracture in the sheer granite slab uplifting from the jungle floor. Their previous position had been high above that very cleft.

The jungle grew to the edges of the elevated face of granite. Creeper vines dangled over the sides and huge fern-fronds branched out into space above swirling currents at the whirlpool's edge. Along the incoming river's banks, palm trees arched from both sides. Their fronds and other jungle flora created a barrier shielding a view of the uplifted earth and the river's entrance into the whirlpool. A traveler's canoe could be suddenly caught in the swirling waters. It would spell disaster for the occupant if it happened to get crossways against that cleft opening in the granite. The force of the water could hold it fast, roll it over or destroy it completely. Truly, this is the end of the river.

Con pointed high up the up-thrust rock and muttered, "See crack." The fissure began as a tiny crack in the granite slab far below where the two men had lain beneath the tree fern. It ran a dog-leg course going downward to the right, then begin to split apart as it turned left continuing downward. The crack opened to a width of two feet as it entered the churning water's surface. Creating a depth of over 40 feet, the excess river water swirled around in an effort to get through that narrow cleft in the rock. Its water was sucked down, eventually to be drawn through a large opening thirty feet below to thereby advance to the opposite side of the granite face. It roiled and churned upwards as it reformed into the shape of a peaceful river, making a wide bend to ultimately disappear underground. The arc of that wide curve had created an inlet as it, over millions of years, eroded away the base of the huge granite upheaval above it. The limestone caves that formed behind the fissured granite face were colossal voids in the decaying remains of ancient foothills approaching the Maya Mountains.

"The canoes are here," Barkow said. "It means there's some way for a man to get behind that granite face."

Con looked at the strength of the river's flow as it rushed against the cleft, some forcing its way through, but the vast majority being sucked downward by a whirlpool of its own making. He abruptly turned, vanished into the jungle, searching until he found where the dugouts had been pulled upon the riverbank. There, he began an extensive search of the area. No bent or broken plant growth escaped his keen eyesight. Eventually he found part of a moccasin track in the mud. Here a small stalk broken, there a bit of moss missing from a fallen tree. The faint sign led him toward an ancient tree growing above a rocky outgrowth where the main trunk had formed huge roots over a squat, upright, granite boulder. They had grown around and over the sides of the stone like a massive nine-fingered hand clutching in a contorted death grip.

Con methodically searched around the rock-grasping root system and there it was. Unseen unless looking directly at it from the proper angle—an opening eight feet tall like an incision between the rock and root. Starting in a mere crack spreading to twenty-two inches in width then narrowing back to a crack. Upon close inspection the root forming one side of the opening appeared slightly worn as if it had been faintly burnished by leather. To Con it could not have been more clearly indicated than if a message had been carved into the root; *People have passed through this opening.* He retraced his steps back to where Barkow still pondered the assault of the river against the cleft granite wall.

"Welcome back." Barkow said. "Find anything interesting?"

"Find way into mountain."

"What!" Barkow exclaimed. "You found a way to get through?"

"Come. Con show." He led Barkow to the opening by the root-bound rock he had discovered. As Barkow inspected the opening Con removed his back pack.

"Barkow big man." Con said. "Con go first. See inside."

"Wait a minute." Barkow said as he fished in a side pocket of his pack. He brought out a small flashlight. "It might be dark in there." He smiled as he handed the light to Con.

"Boss man plenty smart." He said, as he slipped through the narrow space. In a few minutes he called from the opening. "Give backpacks than Boss come." Barkow shoved the backpacks in, one at a time, then stepped into position to wriggle through. It was extremely tight for a man of his size and he had to remove the .357 from its holster and hand it through to Con; whereupon he managed to force his body past the opening. At once he recognized the sound of gurgling water.

Putting on their packs, the two men found the river water flowing from the roiling confusion of getting inside and welling upward. It was dark but for an eerie, silvery light that came through the narrow opening of the cleft in the rock between them and the outside world. They proceeded along the riverbank inside the huge cavity. Where the river began to bend they found an upright, worked block of sandstone called a stela, standing before a tunnel of sorts. Carved deeply into the seven foot stone, almost to the point of being three dimensional, was the symbol of a Mayan Vision Serpent. The ancient serpent image depicted a human head emerging from between the snake's jaws. As the two men discussed the carving, Con explained in broken English that it was believed by ancient Mayans to be the vehicle by which celestial bodies, such as the sun and stars, moved across the heavens. The shedding of a snake-skin also created a powerful symbol of rebirth and renewal. The shaft entrance behind the stela led away at a slightly upward angle. Barkow played the beam of the flashlight around the outside of the tunnel entrance. Surrounding the opening were antique blocks of sandstone cut to shape by builders, hundreds, if not thousands of years in the past. They formed the gaping jaws in the mouth of a serpent's head. The curved fangs, mortared into the stone mouth was made from a pair of elephant tusks.

"That's very odd. No elephants inhabit Mesoamerica." Barkow said. "They could only have come from a foreign vessel, perhaps shipwrecked or a trader. This is an entrance into something that was highly prized by whoever designed this opening." They walked into the tunnel as it curved upward with niches cut at various intervals into the side walls that held images of serpents, carved from sandstone. After a distance of perhaps a hundred feet, the passageway divided at a wye junction becoming two separate tunnels. At the point where they split, was a huge coiled serpent with jade eyes, also carved in sandstone.

They took the right-hand course, not being aware that either direction would bring them to an exit onto the base floor along the side of a steep stairway in a great temple. Approaching the tunnels end they could smell a slight smoky odor and see light reflected on the side walls of their passageway. Barkow turned off his flashlight and cautiously approached the exit. Oil lamps burning in wall sconces attached twenty feet above the temple floor, were spaced at a distance of approximately twenty-five feet apart.

"Do you see or hear anyone in the temple," Barkow said in a hushed voice.

Con shook his head. "No hear," he said.

After watching and listening a few minutes, they slowly ventured out onto the temple floor. The oil lamps sputtered and gave dim, flickering, shadowed light to the temple. Walking out to the center of the sanctuary, they turned back and looked at the design structure from the temple floor. They saw two serpent head entrances, one of which they had just walked out of, at each side of a steep staircase of narrow stone steps rising some eighty feet to an altar platform at the top. The stairs, flanked by the snake-head exits were central to the stepped pyramid design common with all Mayan temples. The majestic structure took up one entire side of the huge cavern, elevated to a height of a hundred feet. At the top of the stairs, behind the altar, stood a small, stone hut-like structure with a single opening. Down each side of the staircase, crawled the corpulent bodies of twin, stone serpents, extending from altar floor to the foot of the stairs. Their snake-heads lay flat, jaws stretched apart, from which human-ized heads protruded with their chins resting upon the temple floor. Above, at the altar, two carved stone idols stood a few feet back on either side. These statues embodied Chaac, the Mayan rain god and the Jaguar god. Before each idol stood a squat, stone pedestal with a shallow bowl carved into its top.

Barkow and Con approached the stone staircase that rose from the temple floor at a severely steep angle. The steps were approximately fifteen feet in width, sixteen inches in height and six inches in depth. Climbing the narrow treads both men saw the dark reddish splotches splattered upon and running down the central part of the staircase, making it obvious that blood sacrifices were held here. At the top stood the stone altar, four feet tall and three wide, shaped with a flattened top. It too, was covered with congealed blood as well as both idols, especially their faces, and the floor. In the stone bowls lay a dried mass of jellied blood.

"Not good." Con muttered as he looked at the stone pedestal bowl before the Jaguar God.

"No." Barkow said. "It's not good at all. This blood can't be more than a few days old."

"Blood from small animal, not man."

Barkow nodded. "Yes, there's not enough to be from a human sacrifice. That stuff on and around the altar has much more and it looks to me like the bleeding body was thrown down the stairway."

"This sacred temple. Only use for blood sacrifice."

"I think you're right Con. This place seems deserted. I wonder; where everyone's at?"

They looked in the small hut-like structure behind the alter, which was empty with the exception of it being located at the exit from a very long, narrow staircase that was so steep it was almost a ladder made of stone. With Con in the lead, they started down the dark, stepped passage. Barkow switched on his flashlight and followed a few steps behind. The bottom of the steps ended at a room no bigger than a closet with a low opening that came out behind the huge coiled serpent at the wye junction of the tunnel they had used coming in.

"This must be the way they bring in the sacrificial hostage." Barkow said.

Con said nothing, but gravely nodded. They took the left tunnel and returned to the temple exiting on the lower floor.

"Let's see if there is a different way out of this place." Barkow said. "You go to the right and I'll go left. We'll meet at the center of the back wall on this floor."

They split up with Barkow walking along the wall of the cavern-temple at his left. He found an entrance opening to an empty room. On the exterior wall by the opening was a carved relief of Chaac, the ancient Mayan Rain God. Chaac, as well as various other Mayan Gods, was depicted by ancient Mayans with both human and animalistic features. In Chaac's case, he was humanized but had some snake-like aspects and fish-like scales. He wore a headdress of an exaggerated design and carried a stone axe. His nose curled and his lower lip jutted outward.

Barkow continued around the wall of the temple, even past the midway point, finding nothing else of interest. After a short way he met Con.

"Hi Con. Find anything?"

"Con nodded. "Find plenty rooms and way to outside."

"Did you find any Indians?" Barkow said.

Nodding slowly, Con said. "Indian village at cave mouth."

They walked back in the direction Con had come along the curvature of the temple wall and came upon a tunnel turning off to the left. This tunnel led in a long curve with openings to what appeared to be storage rooms along both sides. Barkow shone his light into a couple of them which appeared to be empty. Eventually, a new source of light began to slowly increase into a silvery-gray, fog-like appearance and Barkow turned off his flashlight. As they warily moved forward, the tunnel opened into yet another cavern. From where they stood, Barkow could make out a long, low opening of perhaps fifty yards in length. Both ends tapered downward disappearing at ground level. This mouth to the cave appeared to be roughly twelve feet high at its central and highest opening.

Outlined against the outside day-lit jungle were shadowed images of the Indians and their camp. Being inside the cave, they needed no tents or coverings of any kind. A few small campfires with pots hanging from tri-poles above the flames dotted the area. Scattered around were sleeping areas, a few low stools and slightly raised, flat slabs of flagstone. Both men and women were seen. They all wore scant articles of clothing with many, bare above the waist.

To their right, against the rear wall to this cavern, which separated it from the one holding the Serpent Temple, was a building of sorts. With the ceiling of the cave being only twelve feet above the floor, it was a simple chore to build walls from top to bottom with doorways and window openings to form a crude building-like arrangement. The end wall facing Con and Barkow some forty feet to their right, had no openings. The front wall held a doubled door with crossbar, centered in a space of thirty feet. At the end of this space the rest of the structure extended outward another four feet then ran for a distance of some sixty feet, with door and window openings.

Barkow and Con stood at the opening mouth of the tunnel that led back to the Temple of the Serpent in the silvery semi-darkness. Con removed his backpack and handed it to Barkow.

"Boss man wait by big snake where tunnel go two way." He held his hands with palms together at his chest then extended his arms forward while separating the palms wider and wider. "Con look, look then come tell Barkow."

"That's a good plan," Barkow said. "I'll wait for you by the big snake."

The Mayan nodded and slipped away to fade away into the eerie silver light. Barkow, carrying the guide's pack, retraced his steps through the tunnel back to the Temple of the Serpent and entered the mouth of one of the snake-head tunnels. He went to the coiled-snake carving at the wye junction of the tunnel coming from the river to the temple. He stepped behind the huge carving, removed his own backpack and set them both aside. Barkow sat down with his thoughts and waited for Con to return.

Con looks just like the rest of those Indians lounging around the entrance to these caves. He can walk around undetected where I cannot go. I hope I find that Lancair soon and get the hell out of this accursed jungle. I'm missing Laura a lot more than I thought I would. I'd call her right now if the Sat phone could send or receive in this cave. Unless there are more, we know of three huge caverns with tunnels connecting them. I wonder what or who they cut up on that alter and why. Whatever is going on here, I can't leave fast enough.

The time slowly passed.

CHAPTER FOURTEEN

L EAVING BARKOW IN the tunnel, Con sauntered toward a group of Indians who seemed to simply be wasting time around the long, low entrance into the cave. Since he wore only a loin cloth and sandals he looked as much like the others, that no one paid attention to him. He stopped and stood looking out through the long, low exit from inside the cave, to the jungle outside. Since he saw no other Indians on the outside, Con thought it prudent not to go out and draw attention to himself. He made his way along the opening, passing groups and individuals. Some distance from the fires, an elderly woman sat making corncakes. He watched for a moment, then approached and spoke in the Maya tongue; "May a Mayan have a corncake?"

She looked up from her work and appraised him from head to foot.

"I have not looked upon you before," she said, handing him a cake.

"Thank you, Mother. I have not been here very long. May Conchaco set by your fire?"

"Conchaco is welcome to share my fire. Have you returned from a vision quest?"

"No. I come from the jungle."

"Many young men who seek answers from a quest, never return." She looked both ways as if in fear that she had been overheard."

"Do not fear me, Mother," Con said. "I am not here to cause trouble."

"My Son, do you not know what this place is?" She offered another corncake.

"No Mother. I do not."

"This is the tribe of The Jaguars. We lived here in peace until the Aztec," she turned her head and spat, a sign of disrespect, "came. He speaks with a forked tongue."

"What would an Aztec know of Maya Jaguars?"

"He is a vile man who will get us all killed, I think."

"Why do you think so ill of him, Mother?"

"Since he came to us, the Haab' has turned four times. He filled our Leaders heads with ancient stories of when Maya was strong and feared by all. He resurrected the sacrifice of humans. He forces our young men to seek the quest of the Vision Serpent. Those who survive the requirements and have a vision, can then commune with gods of past glory. When they return here, they eat the flesh of those sacrificed to Chaac and become Snake Warriors."

"I know of Chaac, Mother, the ancient Maya god of rain."

"Jaguars who become Snake Warriors worship a reptilian, snake-like Chaac with scales and curved fangs, who demands only the blood of non-Indians."

"Where do they find non-Indians in jungle swamps?"

"The Aztec," she again turned her head and spat, "is connected directly with Chaac through a Medium known as Kortez. That Medium provides the non-Indians to be sacrificed. Our Snakes have prisoners being fattened for their day of sacrifice."

"How can an Aztec contact the medium, Mother?"

"He goes into the jungle, sometimes for days, and by using ancient chants and rites, calls the medium forth. Anyone not knowing the correct order of the rites would die a horrible death if he observed the Aztec communing with the medium."

"I would know more of the Vision Serpent, Mother." Con said quietly.

The old Mayan gave him two corn cakes and a gourd of cool water. "Listen, my child, and learn." She said. "The Vision Serpent is most important of all snakes. It is bearded and has a rounded snout. It often has two heads, one of which is the spirit of a god or ancestor emerging from its jaws. During bloodletting rites, Serpent Warriors_experience visions in which they communicate with their ancestors or gods. These visions take the form of a huge serpent providing a path to the spirit world. The ancestor or god being called emerges from the serpent's mouth. The vision serpent is how ancestors or Gods show themselves to a Maya Serpent Warrior. To them, the Vision Serpent is a direct link between themselves and the gods."

"Thank you, Mother, for your words of instruction. Conchaco would see the humans awaiting sacrifice, if possible."

"They are prisoners in the chamber of the lost, kept in total darkness but fed well to fatten them for sacrifice."

"Where is the chamber of the lost, Mother?"

"It is attached to the rooms of the Aztec which in turn is attached to the hall of the Snake Warriors." The woman looked directly into his face. "Do not follow the snake, my child. Take yourself away from this place."

"This Mayan thanks you, Mother, for your wisdom, your food and your water." Con stood up and faced her. As was his way, he slowly and solemnly nodded to the old woman, then turned and walked away. He reached the side-wall of the great cavern and followed it around, toward the long building he and Barkow had observed when they first looked into this cave. In the semi-darkness of the strange silvery light, he passed a huge pile of drying palm fronds. His natural curiosity made him wonder why they would have a need for palm fronds inside a cavern.

He stopped and looked back at the pile. *What can be the use for such a large amount of palm-fronds?* He thought as he turned and walked back to them. Stacked against the wall of the cavern the fronds lay as they had been placed with the cut ends pointing downward on the stack and the leaf ends laid flat and overlapping each other as they climbed upward. A long loaf of fronds extended from the wall outward and also stretched along the wall on both sides forming the shape of a cross T. Con stood before the pile a moment and then began pulling away some of the fronds. He abruptly stopped and at once began replacing the fronds.

It not good for anyone see Con removing palm fronds. He thought and began walking away toward the makeshift building. There were several door and window openings without doors, gates, curtains or shutters. Con cautiously peered into a window but could make out nothing in the darkness. He thought it to be empty. He walked along the face of the so-called building that was actually just a wall built from cavern floor to the low ceiling. Now and then he looked into a window opening but saw or heard nothing. Near the end of the building he looked in and saw it lighted by several stone oil lamps. It was obviously a living quarters because he saw a sleeping space, several low chairs and matching table but no sign of a person. Next from the interior end wall, set back about four feet, the final thirty feet of building contained a single opening, inset with heavy, wooden, double doors and secured by a long crossbar jammed firmly in place. Con noticed an odd thing. Both doors were lined around their sides, tops and bottom edges with leather strips that apparently made them rain tight. *Rain-tight in a cave where it never rains?* He thought. *That is a very foolish thing.* His brow wrinkled with concentration for a moment then the answer came. *This is where the prisoners awaiting sacrifice are held. The Mother told me they were kept in the dark. Those strips are to keep the light from entering around the doors.* At that moment his keen hearing picked up a low sobbing from inside. As he listened intently he looked around to see if anyone was paying attention to his actions. From the tunnel entrance into this cave, he saw five men walking in single file toward his direction. They each carried a clay pot by a rope handle. Con faded away from the double doors, moving without haste, but back into the Indian camps. He picked a camp that appeared deserted and sat cross-legged before the ashes of a dead fire. With head down, giving the appearance of nodding in sleep, his narrowed eyes watched the four men approach and pass, paying him no attention.

They went directly to the double doors and stopped. They appeared to be waiting for something. Con remained in position, pretending to be asleep.

A while later he noticed two Snake Warriors threading their way through the encampment. Their long, black hair was upswept from the back. It was coated with an ointment that held it together, as if greased or glued. It arched up, above and over the head, blending into a thick coil, ending in front of the forehead. Over this arch of hair, the vivid yellow and black skin of a small snake was stretched, with its complete head still attached and affixed to the end of the arc of hair. The jaws were propped open showing curved fangs, as if it were striking. Small, polished stones replaced the eyes.

The faces of both warriors were tattooed, starting from each side of the nose, the thick, black lines went above and below the warrior's eyes then narrowed and rejoined to form one line, giving the eye-corner a sharply slanted appearance when it became a single line above the ear. The cheeks, adorned with lines that intensified, forming a snake-like expression. A short skirt made of jaguar-skin, their only article of clothing. Each carried a killing-club, carved from hardwood, with the striking ball being formed from a natural knot in the wood, providing strength.

Con watched as the Snake Warriors approached the five men with clay pots. Without stopping, they went straight to the double doors and removed the crossbar, then threw open both doors and went inside. Wailing and bawling began from the prisoners, as the two warriors came back through the doors dragging a small bamboo cage that held a naked man, so cramped he could neither sit nor lie down. His white skin made it obvious he was not of Indian descent.

At once, the Indians with the pots gathered around the cage and began repeating a low, eerie refrain, while dipping strangely carved paddles into the pots. "Ah-ne-oh-oh, ah-ne-oh-oh."

The paddles were about two feet long and carved with symbols along the slim rounded shaft of the handle. The end was carved into a flat rectangle of wood, somewhat like a spatula. The pots contained a thick, dark-green, paint-like liquid. It dripped like pancake batter from the withdrawn paddles. The Indians poked the paddles between the bamboo bars and smeared the green slime on the white man in the cage. He, being so cramped, could do nothing but curse the Indians, to avoid being coated with green.

Con watched, knowing this was ritual, in preparation of a blood sacrifice. When the Snake Warriors went back into the prison for a second cage, he stood and leisurely angled toward the mouth of the tunnel that connected this cavern with that of the snake temple. Once inside he broke into a run to the entrance of the temple. There, he stopped and cautiously inspected the area to make sure no one was about. Deciding it was safe, he quickly ran through the flickering light from the oil lamps and into one of the tunnels to the wye junction. He ducked behind the huge snake carving and stopped short; Barkow stood with the unwavering .357's muzzle pointed straight at him.

"We must leave quick-quick." Con gasped. "They prepare sacrifice. Bring captives here. Take to altar."

"Okay, Con, let's go. We can go back to the river cavern and hide out there."

They started down the tunnel and suddenly halted.

"What's that noise?" Barkow said. "Sounds like singing."

A repeated intonation grew in volume.

"That sound is Mayan chant, we no go this way," Con said

"Come with me." Barkow said as he touched Con's arm, then turned and sprinted back, to jog past the wye and hurry through another passageway. They slid to a stop where it exited into the temple. All appeared unoccupied, therefore they entered and crept along the left side of the temple wall to stop by a dark opening into an empty chamber. A legend of Mayan mythology was carved into the wall next to the opening.

"This is the room of the Rain God." Barkow said. "I came across it when we were checking the temple out."

"Tunnel with storeroom good place to hide." Con muttered, then holding one hand up, standing rock-still, he listened. "Many Indian come through that tunnel to temple." He declared.

"Quick, Con. In here." Barkow yanked the guide into the Rain God's dark empty room. There being no door, they each went to one side of the opening and waited. Hearts pounding, both men now heard the low sing-song refrain, as the Jaguar Tribe spilled into the temple, chanting identical syllables in repetition.

The chant murmured on, gradually growing louder as if someone slowly increased the volume of a hundred speakers. The temple filled with people swaying, back and forth, before the steep stairway to the altar. The refrain echoed and re-echoed in the great cavern. The crowd had grown to a point where the drug induced, mesmerized Indians could but vaguely mimic a swaying motion. For some unknown reason, there remained an unoccupied half-circle of space, ten feet across, before the opening where Barkow and Con crouched. The chant continued to grow in volume, filling the temple with a primeval roar. The clear sound from a conch-shell gave one long, earsplitting blast. As its echo faded away…all other sound had stopped, causing an ethereal silence, clearly immoral, evil and heart-wrenching.

CHAPTER FIFTEEN

IN THE DEADLY silence, a distant, tinkle of sound was remotely heard. Its volume gradually welling up, echoing the soothing undertone of shaken maracas, unrefined and vulgar, as a single file of Snake Warriors entered the temple. Tied above the left knee of each warrior were rattlesnake rattles, earned in that man's first successful vision quest. They chinked in unison as each man's left foot trod upon the temple floor.

The crowd divided, leaving an open path through its midpoint, from the center of the stairway's base to the rear of the sanctuary. The soft chink—chink—chink continued as the path from stairs to back wall filled up. Those warriors continued marching in place, maintaining a cadenced pulse as their followers spread across the cavern's back wall and then turning both left and right down along each flank of the silent crowd. On the side where Chaac's consecrated chamber was located, that mystical, half-circle of empty floor space before the entrance, remained vacant as the line of Snake Warriors physically forced the crowd back, in order to get past without stepping in the hallowed zone. When all warriors were in place the chinking sound echoed off the walls until a second pitch from the conch sounded; at once a tranquility filled the temple. Barkow and Con observed the spectacle taking place, from the sanctified room of the Rain God.

In the dead silence, all faces turned upward to the top of the stairway, staring at the splendidly carved image of Chaac. Suddenly, the effigy burst into glorious life. A fire pit in the floor before the stone image held a bed of live coals. When a certain pitched-laced wood was pushed upon them, flames flared up creating a unique orange glow upon the statue, changing it to a rich color of antique gold. The stone image of the tribe's Jaguar God turned green, lighted up by the same manner and appearing to pulsate in the flickering light of the oil lamps.

Billowing clouds of greenish-gold smoke filled the space before the sacrificial altar. The Aztec's form slowly appeared as the smoke drifted apart, legs spread with both arms raised. His right hand held a knife made from a piece of obsidian; half its length chipped into a wide, razor-sharp, double edged blade. The balance was worked into a handle, bound with a tightly wound leather thong wrapped about it, creating a slip-proof grip. The Aztec's hideous face, painted to produce horror, stared from a hooded mantle made of jaguar skin that draped across his shoulders. The cat's head-skin created the hood on his forehead. Huge disks of jade were attached to his earlobes. His long, black hair bushed wildly around his face.

Five naked men came from the single opening of the hut. Two stood left, two right and one knelt at the head of the altar. The Aztec brought arms down and feet together and held the knife handle with both hands before his solar-plexus, blade pointing to his chin. In the unearthly silence he began a low, slow chant; ah...ne...oh...oh—ah...ne...oh...oh. Here and there, like a contagious disease, the silent crowd began to pick up the chant. Others joined as the mantra grew flamboyant and vulgar. The syllables came more rapidly as the Indians began connecting and slurring them together into a single word, ahneeohcho. At the top platform two Snake Warriors came out of the hut-like structure, half carrying and half dragging a naked white man, splattered with dark green splotches over much of his body. Having been cramped in a cage for a long period he could hardly bend his joints; his screaming was drowned out by the frenzied, hysterical people now repeatedly yelling, ahneeohcho, AHN-EEOHCHO!

The Warriors handed off the misshapen man to the five naked men. Four of which took hold of an extremity and pulled the senseless babbling victim out flat then swung him upon the altar, face up; they stretched his arms and legs out and down. The kneeling man at the head of the altar holding each end of a length of leather strap, slipped it under the captive's chin and forced his head down over the end of the altar. This position caused his chest to be brutally forced upward. The Aztec priest brought the razor sharp point of the obsidian blade to off center, on the victim's chest, at a location between two ribs over the heart. With a swift slash across the chest, he cut through skin and meat between the ribs and then pushed the flat blade in and twisted, prying the living rib bones apart, exposing the beating heart. He reached in, gripped the throbbing organ and ripped it loose from the chest cavity, trailing arteries still spurting blood upon the priest and holders alike, then held it up and out to the people below, which signaled the insane shouting "AHNEEO-HCHO" to abruptly stop, creating an eerie silence.

The body of the victim, still oozing blood, was heaved out over the stairway to the temple floor where it fell on the steep stone steps with a muted thud, then rolled and flopped, with flailing arms and legs, down the stairs to the floor of the temple. Warriors, assigned to the job, amputated the arms, legs and head, giving them to the Snake Warriors in the center line, who at once began passing the severed appendages back up the line of warriors.

The Aztec held the dripping heart out to the assembly below, then stepped over and ground it against the face of the Chaac effigy, crushing it to bloody pulp as blood ran down the statue's front, then placed the mangled remains in its carved stone pedestal bowl.

In the utter silence the blood soaked Aztec priest once more began the low chant; "ah...ne...oh...oh," and the crowd, sporadically began taking up the sacrificial mantra and a second terrified victim was brought forth, destined to go through the same ritual as the first.

At the end of the second sacrifice, the fires before the two effigies were extinguished. The victim's body parts were passed warrior to warrior back up the line and into a storeroom off the tunnel leading to the residential cavern. The warriors began to file back, in synchronized step, to their rooms in the Indian camp cavern. After the chinking tempo of their snake rattles had died away, the remaining Indians returned through the storeroom tunnel to the community cavern, leaving the temple empty of humanity. The blood on altar and floor at the top of the stairs, was congealing, producing a lingering, rusted iron smell and taste in the air. Barkow and Con remained hiding in the room dedicated to the ancient Rain God of the Mayans.

They eventually decided no one lingered in the temple and cautiously stepped out, looked around and headed for the tunnel leading to the wye junction. As they approached the gaping mouth of the snake-head tunnel near the base of the stairs, they stopped.

"This is where they dismembered those poor devils." Barkow said. "I wonder why they cut them up that way."

"Save parts to eat," Con said. "Torsos go to jungle, feed wildlife.

Trying not to step in coagulating pools of blood in front of the tunnel, they made their way to the wye junction and on through the tunnel to the interior river cavern.

"I'm glad to get away from that God-awful smell of blood."

"Me no like blood smell." Con said as they walked together. "Con has much to tell Boss of what find."

"First let's get outside in the fresh air." Barkow said. "I need to see blue sky and sunshine. We now know this entire cave is made of three huge caverns, connected by tunnels."

After washing hands and splashing river water in their faces, they returned to the root-bound rock entrance and exited the cave. Con led the way into the jungle and at a safe distance, in the cool, shady darkness by a small stream, he halted. When a simple camp was set up, both men lay with their packs as pillows and Con began to speak.

"Con can find entrance mouth into Indian Camp cavern from here."

"Did you go through the mouth to the outside?"

"It no safe." Con related all that he saw and did while scouting the residential cavern, leaving out the pile of palm fronds.

"You did a damn good job of finding out what's going on. It's obvious that Aztec priest is using his knowledge of ancient lore to control the Jaguar tribe."

Con sat up in a cross legged position and began to speak. "Corncake woman say Kortez medium provide white captives. Hah!" Con turned his head and spat on the ground.

"I was sure the Cortes drug cartel was somehow tied up in this operation." Barkow also sat up. "How the Lancair fits into what is going on, I don't know."

"Con know," he said.

Barkow's sharp gaze swung to the guide. "What does Con know?"

"Con know airplane."

"Con should know. We've been on the trail of the damned thing since we came into the jungle. Why is Con smiling?"

"Con happy," stated the jungle guide.

I have never seen Con in a happy mood. I wonder what he's holding back. It's obvious now that he knows something he has not told me yet.

"And, why is my friend Con so happy?" Barkow said.

"Con find big pile palm fronds in cavern."

"I think Con found some joy juice and drank it without saving any for his friend Barkow."

"Con no drink happy juice," the guide said and turned his face away from Barkow.

"I do not think my friend Con looked at palm fronds. I am sure he has been drinking jungle juice and did not save any for boss man Barkow."

Con remained silent keeping his face turned away.

"Maybe Con find woman to make him happy. I think a woman and jungle juice has made my friend very happy and now he won't look at me because he knows I'll see he's not telling his friend about it. Did Con and the woman have fun in the pile of palm fronds?"

Con turned around and for the first time, Barkow heard him laugh. He roared with laughter and rolled on the ground. "Boss man plenty smart," he howled with laughter.

"What woman made Con happy," Barkow said.

"No. No woman, Boss." Tears ran down his face as he could hardly control his hilarity. "No joy juice. Con see airplane Boss search for. It in cavern under palm fronds."

"You mean it's there? The plane is in the cave?"

"Yes Boss. Plane in cave. Con look-look little bit. No want Snake Indian see Con at plane. Hurry-hurry go away."

"Thank you, my friend. Con is a good jungle guide, good cave guide and a damn good friend." He seized the guide's hand and pulled them closer together, then shook it as he looked into Con's face. Barkow possessed a preternatural stare which could lock on a person's eyes in a near physical grip. The Mayan guide at once felt its controlling pressure. He knew Barkow was conveying something exceptional to him.

"Barkow good friend," Con said in a grave voice. After a long moment he felt a release, as if an invisible link had been broken. From that instant, he realized, he had a connection with Barkow that could never be severed. They had bonded as surely as father to son or brother to brother.

"Thank you Con. To have you for a friend is an honor I cherish."

They both remained silent as they sat in the tropical greenwood. After a while Barkow spoke.

"I wish I could go into that cavern to see the plane, but they would spot me right away. Do you feel comfortable going in there again?"

"It okay. Con can go. All they see is Indian."

"What does Con think is most important to do?"

Con pondered the question for a while before he spoke.

"Do Barkow want save airplane?"

"No. My job was to find it. I want to save the captives."

"To save captives need plenty man."

"I know. I just don't know how to get them here."

"Con know."

"What does Con know?"

"Con know how get many man help."

"How would Con do that?"

"Con call Belize Police. Use Boss man's Satellite radio."

"They would not come."

"Con call, they come."

"They would laugh at you, Con. They would not come."

"No laugh. Con and Police, friends. Con call, they come."

"Yeah, I bet. How many could you get to come here?"

"How many Boss man want?"

Barkow's thoughts quickly analyzed the situation. *Hummm, there are two ways into the three caverns interconnected by tunnels. The low opening to the tribal cavern and the root-bound rock entrance to get behind the whirlpool into the river cavern. The tribe must have around three hundred people plus the thirty or so captives. About eighty of the tribe have been converted into Snake Warriors. It would take around a hundred troops to adequately grab all of them in one clean stroke.*

Barkow smiled. "A hundred men with full combat gear."

"When time right, Con get hundred man with gear."

Barkow realized now that Con was dead serious in what he was saying. He looked hard at his friend and the little Mayan stared back.

"One Hundred. With combat gear?"

The Mayan simply nodded his head as he stared at Barkow.

"Why would they come if you called?"

"Con and Police friends."

"We could give them the lat/long position. How long would it take them to get here through the jungle?"

"Maybe two hour?"

"What!" Two hours my foot. Incredulous." Barkow ridiculed.

Con held up his hand with all digits splayed. "Five," he said.

"Five what?"

"Five whap-whap," then pointed his right index finger up making little circles, "Twenty man each."

"You're serious, aren't you Con."

Once more the jungle guide simply stared at Barkow, nodding slowly and Barkow believed, with all his heart and soul, Con could get a hundred men with all their gear to come, if he called. The two men began to discuss how such a raid could take place.

"We would need the Jaguar tribe out of the cavern to rescue the captives." Barkow said. I don't want to wait until they have another sacrifice.

"Captive need know we come."

"Yes they would but how can you get in to tell them?"

"Con have plan."

"Damn it," Barkow exclaimed. "I wish I could help."

"Boss man help after Con talk captives."

"Okay. Where should I wait for you?"

"Boss man wait where first see river end."

"On that ledge above the whirlpool, right?"

Again came the slow, somber nod, now recognized as the way Con pledged truth and agreement.

"How soon can you talk to the captives?"

"Con go now. Barkow wait."

"Why can't I wait here, in this camp?"

"Too close to secret way into temple. Indian snake-man plenty smart fella."

"Okay Con. I'll wait above the whirlpool."

Barkow stood and put on his backpack. "You ready?" He said.

"Boss go now. Con go too."

Barkow noticed Con still sat upon the ground as the reason flashed into his mind.

Apparently Con wants me to leave first. I wonder what sort of plan he has, but if he has one and don't want to talk about it, so be it. I'd trust that man with my life.

With those thoughts on his mind, he turned and headed for the place where they had first looked upon the whirlpool at the river's end.

After Barkow left, Con stood and slipped into his backpack.

He very carefully checked all around the site of their makeshift camp looking closely at every bush and hanging tree limb, especially those around where they had come through the jungle into this location. Satisfied that there were no bent or broken branches, tracks or other tell-tale signs to show they passed that way, he chose a broad, four foot fern frond and eased it from the ground, pulling up even its shallow root. He went to where they had lain in the grass and swept the flattened grass blades into an upright position. He backed out the way they had come in, sweeping with the frond until he was beneath a large tree, the ground covered with undisturbed twigs and tree litter, then crept away to the root-bound rock entrance of the cavern. Searching about the area, Con found a small, rocky outcropping in the jungle floor. He carefully removed a few larger rocks and created a depression in which he placed his backpack and the fern frond. With the skill of an artist he replaced the rocks he had removed and inspected it with a critical eye. Feeling assured no one would notice any change he returned to the entrance of the cavern and disappeared inside.

CHAPTER SIXTEEN

CON PAUSED WITHIN the dark entrance of the river cavern, the first in a linked chain of three they had discovered. He waited patiently until his eyes became accustomed to the strange, silvery light. He heard no sound except the gurgling action of the river-water welling upwards from the depths. He walked past the stela and strode through the fabricated snake-head entrance of the tunnel, leading to the separation junction providing separate entries into the temple. He chose the right hand branch of the wye in order to enter on the opposite side from where the bodies of the two sacrificed victims had been dismembered.

The scent of clotting blood was still dominant as he hastened across the sanctuary and into the tunnel of store-rooms. His sense of smell immediately led him to the correct room. Inside, by the dim light of a single oil-lamp flame, he discovered two large clay pots of water holding the hands, feet, arms and legs of the recent victims. They had been cut roughly into eight-inch lengths. He saw several tables and a long tier of three shelves dug into the storeroom's rear wall. Lined along the top ledge was thirty-nine skulls in various stages of decomposition. The last two were the fresh heads of today's victims, upon which blind cave-rats were feeding.

Con left the storeroom and looked into each of the remaining rooms opening off the tunnel. All except four were empty. One contained the skulls and body parts, another held an estimated six hundred blocks of neatly packaged cocaine. In a different room were bales of marijuana stacked floor to ceiling. Woven baskets full of onetime-use packets of heroin, were found in a fourth room.

After checking those storerooms, Con stood at the tunnel's entrance into the residential and final cavern. He waited until it appeared no one was looking in his direction then sauntered out among the encampments in search of the corncake woman's fire. He found it, as before, on the outskirts, away from the other campsites.

"Greetings, Mother," he said as he approached her fire.

"Greetings Conchaco." She said. "Please join my fire."

"Thank you, Mother." He sat cross-legged before the small fire and watched as she began making more corncakes.

"Are you hungry, Conchaco? She said as she looked askance at him, head cocked to one side.

"I have not eaten since this morning."

She filled a gourd with cool water and handed it to him along with two corncakes. "What has Conchaco learned since we last talked?"

"Thank you, Mother," he said. "I have learned the *Jaguar* tribe holds dark secrets." He began, munching on a corncake.

"As dark as the hole from which the Aztec," she turned her head and spat, "crawled."

"If you are unhappy here, why do you stay?"

"I am an old woman. This camp is far from any place that would welcome an old woman. I would perish in the jungle."

"Do you not have a relative to give you aid?"

"No. My man was sacrificed for speaking his thoughts."

"My heart fills with sorrow." Con said, as he looked about her camp and noticed several baskets of pre-made corncakes. "For whom do you make the corncakes?"

"They are to feed the captives awaiting their time of sacrifice. When they had my husband in there, I would take him corncakes. Now the Aztec," again she turned and spat, "forces me to do it for all captives. He has made me understand if I do not feed them, I will join them."

"Do you distribute the food to each captive?" Con asked with interest.

"Why does Conchaco want to know about this?"

"Why did the Mother tell me of it?"

"Because this old woman knows Conchaco is more than a boy of the jungle. In Conchaco's eye shines the light of both suspicion and trust."

"I am suspicious of everyone, Mother, until I know them."

"As am I, Conchaco. I give the cakes with the help of two deaf men, who love each other as a man loves a woman. They also live under the threat of sacrifice if they do not help."

"When do you feed the captives?"

"In middle night, when the people sleep, we feed and water the captives."

"You and the two men?" For answer the old woman simply nodded.

"I would see these men, Mother."

"Come to my fire when all is silent, Conchaco, and you will see them."

"Thank you, Mother. I'll watch for them." Con stood up and faded away from the camp. He worked his way slowly, over to the huge pile of palm fronds. No one paid him any attention; it was far from any firelight. He crept to the T-shaped pile's armpit and dropped to his knees. Moving aside a few fronds he crawled into the pile, coming almost at once to the fuselage of the plane where the trailing edge of the wing attached. He wriggled into the space beneath the wing and lay full length to await the feeding time of the captives.

Several hours later, Con watching from the seclusion of the palm fronds, saw two slender, short men walking hand in hand, as they approached the cake-maker's low fire. On arrival they seated themselves on the ground. The woman put a tiny bundle of small twigs and dry grass on the live coals and the flames at once flashed up for a few seconds then quickly died down.

Con understood this was done on purpose to allow him

to see the two men. They were shaved of all hair and had been coated with some sort of grease to make their nakedness shine in the firelight. They sat holding hands as Con approached out of the darkness. Light from the coals showed highlights of their features, lending a grotesque appearance. The skinny helper's eyes were large, blank, yet filled with fear. Even their eyebrows had been shaved away. They were splattered with splotches of white paint which canceled out the shine in those places.

When Con entered the low firelight the two naked men hugged each other and crouched as if they could make themselves smaller. They were literally shaking with fear.

"Do not fear this man," the woman said. "He is here to help feed and water the captives as ordered by the high priest."

"Greetings," Con said. "I will not harm you."

Their large eyes stared at him as they clung to each other, chest to chest and cheek to cheek.

"They cannot answer, Conchaco. Their tongues have been cut out."

"How do they eat, Mother?"

"I make a thick corn gruel which they drink. It is now time to go. There will be no light. The captives must remain in total darkness at all times. Their cages are set in three rows of ten. I will lead you to the first cage in the front row and you will have to find your way to the rest. Each cage has a bracket holding a water vessel which you fill by using a special dipper of water. Conchaco will take two bags of water. We will bring the corncakes"

They gathered their burdens and headed toward the house of the lost. Con set his woven-waterproof buckets down before the double doors. The only lock was a cross-bar which he lifted away. He flung open both doors and was overwhelmed by the stench that flowed out of the room. He picked up the water and the old woman's hand guided him to the first cage in total darkness. She took his hand and placed it at the corner of the cage and had him touch the bracket holding the mug.

"Thirty cages, some empty. Fill all cups." She moved away

leaving him with the sounds of moaning, weeping and begging from the captives. He dipped water into the mug at each cage and leaned close.

"American?" he would ask. His answer was usually a half sob, half groan.

Feeling his way to the next cage, the process was repeated, and the next, and the next. At the fifth cage he received an answer. "I'm English."

"Rescue come quick-quick. Be brave." Con moved on through the process through the first and second row giving the same answer to anyone who spoke to him. In the third cage of the last row he found success.

"American?"

"I am American. Can you get me out of here?" A male voice sobbed in the darkness.

"You name?"

"Gary Appleton," He whimpered. "Can you take me with you?"

"Rescue come quick-quick. Be brave."

"No! Get me out of this cage." Appleton demanded in a loud voice.

"Shh. Rescue come soon."

Con moved on to the next, and next. In the ninth cage of the row he found her.

"American?"

"Yes, I'm American. Thank God you found us."

"Rescue come quick-quick. Be brave. You name Rawnee?"

"Yes. I am Roni. Are you from Barkow?"

"Me Con. Barkow friend. Rescue soon. You no die." He reached through the bamboo bars of the cage and patted her back. "Be brave, Rawnee."

The next and last cage held an Englishman who said he heard what was said to Roni and thanked Con for his bravery. Con found his way back to the opening where his three companions waited.

The two naked men quickly departed. Con and the woman made their way back to her camp carrying the empty baskets.

"Thank you, Mother, for helping Conchaco."

"You are welcome, Conchaco. Will you rescue the captives?"

"They will be rescued," he said as they sat before the fire.

"How will you do such a thing?"

"I do not know, Mother. Will you help?"

"I will help, Conchaco. When rescue take place?"

"It will happen just before the sun rises tomorrow. Many warriors with guns will charge from the jungle through the long opening into this cave. Move your camp close to cavern wall near the hill of palm fronds to be safe and I will find you. Tell no one"

"Thank you, Conchaco. I will do as you say."

"Good. I must leave now to meet with my warriors." Con stood up and hurried away in the direction of the exit into the jungle. As soon as he was far enough away so she would not notice, he turned to his left, moving silently through the camp of sleeping Indians. At the Chamber of the Lost he turned down along the continuous wall, passing the Aztec's rooms and the Snake Warriors quarters and then veered to the pile of palm branches. He wriggled beneath the fronds being careful to replace those he disturbed while getting in. He sat beside the fuselage at the rear of the plane with his forearms leaning on a horizontal stabilizer of the tail section and watched the Indian camp through a narrow opening he'd made at eye level.

I will know soon if the corncake woman can be trusted. Con thought. *If she has told my plan to the Aztec there will soon be signs of them getting ready to repel an attack at sunrise which is a few hours away. The Snake Warriors in camp now sleep in their quarters. If all remains quiet until the sun rises ... then she is trustworthy.*

Con remained hidden in the fronds watching the camp. Soon he saw the old woman walking in the darkness toward the cavern wall to his right. She carried her baskets, fire tripod and blankets, obviously moving her camp as Con had suggested.

He turned his gaze left, toward the Snake quarters. Across the Indian camps all remained quiet with no one moving about.

Aztec is poor leader, Con thought. *He like the thrill of sacrificing helpless people but has become complacent in his power. The people here are only to be used, but not led. He places no night guards at the entrances of his domain. They have not been challenged by anyone for years and have grown soft and lax. These caves are some sort of supply depot for drugs and the Aztec uses ancient rites and rituals to control.*

The sun rose and with it the darkness changed into that odd silver light. The old woman made a small fire and at once began making more corncakes. Con slipped out of his hiding place and approached the woman.

"Good morning, Mother," he said. She did not answer but kept pounding raw meat into a mashed state which in turn was added to the cornmeal dough and formed into cakes, by hand. A square piece of iron had been placed on four rocks to form a cooking surface above the fire. She hooked two fingers into a small basket and brought out a glob of fat which in turn was dropped onto the heated iron. Uncooked corncakes, laced with meat, were placed upon the makeshift griddle. Finely the woman looked at Con.

"It is not a good morning," she muttered. "Why does Conchaco speak to a useless, old woman with his forked tongue? Where are your warriors?

"It is a wonderful morning, Mother. Birds sing in the trees and Conchaco is very happy."

She turned her head and spat, then flipped each corncake over.

"Mother," he said. "Conchaco is happy because you expected my warriors to come screeching into camp. Now you believe Conchaco lied to you."

"I thought the gods had given this old woman a gift. Life is cruel."

Con smiled. "Your god has not forsaken you, Mother. He has blessed you and the captives. My tongue was forked, but only in making a test. I did not know if you were true or false. Had the

Snake Warriors prepared for a battle…false. Had they slept like the fat, lazy men they are…true.

The old woman, slowly got to her feet and came to Con. She put her arms around him and hugged him to her. Tears of joy ran down her cheeks. "Forgive a foolish, old woman, Conchaco. Please forgive this one."

"Mother forgiven. She right to believe I lied. Conchaco is happy because he wanted Mother to be true."

"Were you my son, I could not love you more. I have been told there will be a great happening at sunrise in four turns of the sun. Today first turn."

"What will happen?"

"All the captives, including me and the boys, are to be sacrificed to the gods. A feast will be made of our flesh. Visiting Gods from other tribes, like the Jaguars, will arrive and all members of our tribe must take part in the feast."

"How will visitors get here Mother, for the happening?"

"They will be brought by the gods during the third turn of the sun."

"I go now, Mother, plan rescue. It be soon. Conchaco will save you."

"Go, Conchaco. May the gods protect you."

Conchaco faded into the silvered shadows. He ambled along, head down, passing through the awakening camps of Indians, unnoticed, unchallenged, meandering toward the tunnel of storerooms that led to the cavern of the temple.

CHAPTER SEVENTEEN

Iɢʜ ᴀʙᴏᴠᴇ ᴛʜᴇ swirling water of the whirlpool, Barkow lay concealed within a thicket of broad-leafed plants and fern growing to the very edge of the sheer drop-off. No ray of morning sunshine penetrated his location. The sunrise sounds of jungle-birds chirping and calling was building into a raucous racket. He'd waited sixteen hours for Con to return. Dozing again, he ignored the bird's clamor until he abruptly became aware and alert. His eyes snapped open and he listened intently, holding his breath. There! It came again, a sound foreign to the jungle. The bubbling, buzzing call of a Bluebird, detached itself from the ordinary sounds of the tropical forest. With a sigh of relief, he gave forth an exact replica of the Bluebird call. In a few minutes Con wriggled in beside him.

"Greetings, Con."

"It good to see my friend. I have much to tell."

"I've grown old waiting for your return. Tell me all."

Con sat beside his friend and told everything he had done and seen, plus all the corncake woman had said to him.

"Today is the first turn of the sun." Barkow said. "If the visitors come on the third turn, that means we have today and tomorrow to hatch a plan and put it in place."

"I think visitors be white man." Con said. "Them with the Cortes drug gang. Mother say gods bring visitor through air." The guide was staring at Barkow and nodding his head. "It gonna be wap-wap bird," he stated.

"I think you're right and they'll either be bringing drugs in or taking them out, but where can it set down here in the jungle?"

"Con will find place where it land."The little jungle guide said.

"While you're at it find a place for those five helicopters with your hundred men in full combat gear to land also."

"No need big space. Give Sat phone to Con, please."

Barkow handed him the phone. "I'll show you how to get a wave band."

"Con know." He said as he began setting up the phone-call while Barkow stared at him in astonishment.

The jungle guide punched in a series of numbers and put the phone on speaker.

"Belize Police Department, Jungle Patrol, Officer Gillmore speaking."

"This Conchaco, Gilly. Please connect to Major."

"Hi Conchaco," Gillmore said. "Will do." A short burst of static sounded.

"Major Bohannan."

"Major this Conchaco. We find Cortes secret hideout in jungle. We have drug case cracked. Barkow and I need one hundred trained Jungle Patrol Commandos, in full combat gear to repel from helicopters to capture approximately three hundred Indians. 100 passive, 200 savage-aggressive. They must arrive at lat/long position I give later this day, maybe tomorrow. It be near this location. He rattled off the co-ordinates for the whirlpool.

"Will we need any special equipment?"

"I think they gonna be all wrapped up with pink bow on top. It very important troops land at precise time, exactly on minute I give later."

"Thanks Sargent Conchaco, I'll get things started at this end and wait for your call."

"Conchaco go hurry-hurry now."Con clicked off and handed the phone to Barkow.

"So you work with the Belize Police." Barkow said. "Why didn't you tell me sooner?"

"It need to know situation."

"Okay, Sargent Conchaco." Barkow said with a grin. "For

holding out on me you owe Boss-man a dinner when we get back to Belize City and I want the biggest steak we can find."

A smile tugged at one corner of his lips as the little guide nodded his head and muttered, "Maybe home-burger."

"I think we should locate that long mouth-opening of the cave first, then see if we can pick up the trail to the landing site."

"Boss man think like jungle guide now," Con said. "Plenty smart."

"Let's go, Con. You can show me how to find a landing place."

The two friends gathered their gear and Con struck off through the jungle with Barkow trailing along behind. They tramped around pineapple bushes and through undergrowth with shiny leaves of all sizes, shapes and shades of green.

Sounds of bird calls, monkey hoots and grunts of unseen animals added to their own heavy breathing at times, combined with the slithering whisper of branch and leaf brushing against them as they moved through small clearings and brief penetrating rays of sunlight. The stuffy, warm air combined with the heavy, natural plant odor and rotting vegetation left a thick, stale taste on Barkow's tongue.

Con turned left and followed a game trail downhill through dripping water and hanging moss, past twisted ropes of vine that spiraled tree-trunks. The daylight darkened and raindrops fell, splattering leaves, quickly growing to monsoon proportions and instantly soaking the two men. Normal sounds of the jungle ebbed into silence. When the ground leveled out, the game trail disappeared. Barkow, slogging on spongy ground cushion beneath the trees, stopped to adjust his pack to a more comfortable position. He noticed a line of leaf-cutter ants, ignoring the rain and marching on a branch close by. He peered between the thick vine-choked trunks and dripping green leaves, looking for the guide, he realized only the unbroken jungle stared back at him giving no clues to which way Con had gone.

Barkow began to hurry through the lush vegetation, wet leaves slapping at his face and body as ground creepers threatened to cause tripping. "This won't do." He muttered and stopped. At once he gave the buzzing call of Bluebird and waited. No answer as the rain beat a tattoo on broad vegetation. Again and louder he gave the call. This time it was repeated and presently Con appeared among the dripping foliage.

"Boss man tired, want rest?" He asked.

"No. I don't want to rest." Grumbled Barkow.

"Why stop?"

"I wanted to shine my shoes."

"Ahh." Con walked on the squishy, rain-soaked ground around Barkow, inspecting him.

"Boss man plenty good lookin' fella, now." He said.

"Con is a wise guy and now owes Boss man big steak dinner and… a bottle of bourbon."

"Maybe home-burger and Coca-Cola."

"Lets go, Con. I don't wanna stand in the rain all day."

"Boss man try keep up." Con said in a cheerful voice as he strode away.

The rain eventually stopped and the tropical sunshine dried off the upper canopy of the jungle in minutes. The two men walked single file with Con in the lead.

"You know what I've been thinking, Con?"

"What Boss man think?"

"Maybe instead of just a clearing to land a helicopter, they have a clearing with camouflage webbing covering it. That way we would not have seen it from the air when we flew in with Vito."

"Aye!" Con blurted. He stopped and turned to face Barkow. "That why we walk round and round." He mumbled. "No find clearing. It probably close to cave mouth."

"Well, we never did find the mouth."

"We pass close to mouth but Con stay away on purpose. Search big circle round cave."

"You found the mouth to the cavern? Why didn't you tell me?"

"It need to know situation." Con said cheerfully.

"We need to get in closer." Barkow said.

"Boss man be plenty smart fella." Con muttered. "Me find quick-quick now.

Within an hour and a half they had located a clearing with camo covering. Con called in the lat/longs and said he would give them the exact time to arrive as soon as a plan was decided on. They returned to the place above the whirlpool to plot their next move. After resting, discussing strategy and eating a camp ration meal, Con hurried back to the Jaguar Tribe's camp to find the Corncake woman.

CHAPTER EIGHTEEN

SHE HAD FOUR fires going with iron slabs across each one.

"Greetings, Mother. I see you make many corncakes."

"Greetings, Conchaco. I am to prepare corncakes all through this day and the next. The Snake Warriors bring baskets of stone-ground corn and cooked meat to pound into the cakes. They provided the meat and rendered fat from the two recently sacrificed men and this iron to cook them on."

"Have you been saved from sacrifice, Mother?"

"No. The two deaf boys and I are to be confined in the dark cages tomorrow at sundown. All captives will be tied by the neck to poles and put in a sacrificial line before sunrise. The first sacrifice will take place as the sun casts its first ray on the jungle treetops."

"Do not live in fear, Mother. You and all captives will be rescued from the line of sacrifice before the sun awakes. What is the Aztec's plan for tomorrow?"

"Tomorrow the Snake Warriors will all go into the jungle and seek a vision. They will not eat anything but the sacred vision-food of the gods. They are not to return to the temple until sundown where they will gorge on dance and rape until the night-sun is directly overhead. Then they will force every living Jaguar Indian into the temple to sing and celebrate until the Snake warriors enter in sacrificial dance and the first sacrifice takes place."

"Who brings the captives out to line them up?"

"It will be the five holders for sacrifice, the Aztec and four Snake Warrior Captains."

"Where will the visitors be during the sacrifices?"

"Twelve of the Kortez Gods are to be in places of honor at the foot of the temple stairs."

"Conchaco thanks you, Mother. Without your knowledge the rescue could not take place. You will be my honored guest when the Aztec and his Snake Warriors are either dead or in prison."

"What will happen to the Jaguar Tribe, Conchaco?

"They may continue to live in the old way, providing they obey the law of the Belize Police Jungle Patrol. No Sacrifices, no killing humans, no killing animals except for subsistence."

"Thank you, Conchaco."

"I am sorry you must go in the cages and the line, but the plan will not work without it."

"It is alright. I will rejoice when you set us free, my son."

He held the old woman in a tender hug for a long moment. "Be well Mother. I will see you after we have the Aztec in chains," he whispered.

"May the gods give you success, my son." She whispered in return.

Sargent Conchaco, of the Belize Jungle Patrol, casually strolled away through the strange silvery light on his way out of the Tribe's Residence Cavern.

⊙ WHEN THEY MET Con told Barkow all the corncake woman had said and they discussed it until all angles of the plan was perfectly clear to both of them.

"It's settled then," Barkow said and repeated for the last time, the sequence of steps the Aztec's plan would take according to what the old woman had told Con.

"Once the Snake Warriors come back at sunset from their vision quest, they will begin to dance around the central fire in the camp of the Jaguar Tribe. This is known as the rape-dance and is performed at the close of each vision quest, prior to the human sacrifice. As they execute the frenzied steps of the dance, building their lust, one by one they peel off the shouting and screaming circle of senseless dancing maniacs in search of any woman they desire. They will be stoned on drugs and not having eaten for twenty-four hours, will be in a nasty mood."

Con's dark eyes flashed in anger as he listened.

"No woman is exempt and must submit to whatever the warrior demands, until shortly before the moon is directly overhead. Just before midnight, they will give drugs to each member of the Jaguar Tribe and herd them into the temple, placing guards over them so none can leave. Then all the Snakes, except the guards in the temple, will wait in their rooms behind the wall in the Residence Cavern."

Con watched Barkow, who continued to sum up the plan of action, gently nodding his head in agreement.

"Shortly after the tribe is secured in the temple, they will form up and do the sacrificial dance with rattlesnake rattles. When all are stamping their left foot in time making the ominous chink-chink-chink of the rattles, they will file into the temple and encircle the people of the Jaguar Tribe. As quickly as the Snake warriors have departed the Tribe's residential cave and entered the temple, the Aztec and five holders will begin bringing the captives out and lining them up, in order to march them up the back stairway of the sacrificial alter.

"At this time the four Captains of the Snake Warriors who also help during the sacrifices will come in through the root-bound rear entrance through the River Cavern and make sure all people are flushed out of the tunnels and into the temple. Then, they will uncover the opening of the secret tunnel from the Aztecs rooms to the wye. They will also help with the captives, many of whom will be unable to walk after being compactly caged in the dark since the time of their capture. The Four Captains will check the camp grounds for stragglers. Two will lead the line of pole-bound captives and two will bring up the rear, following the last pole."

Con, still nodding in agreement, said, "Camp be empty when last captives go into the secret tunnel to back entrance stairs of temple, behind big carved serpent at wye."

"Right," Barkow said. "That's the exact moment your troops need to land. The area should be deserted and they can come in through the mouth of the cave right on the heels of the last pole of captives leaving."

"I'll put twenty man in tunnel from camp to temple," Con Muttered, "twenty man in each tunnel from wye to temple and twenty will go up same steps as captives used, freeing them one at a time."

"Right," Barkow said, "and at that same time I'll bring twenty men through the root-bound entrance to the river cavern."

Con said. "I tell Major the plan."

"Yes Con, it's a good plan. We'll have them all pinned down in one place and can take out the Aztec, the Snake Warriors and the Mayan tribe, all at one time. The key is to have a large enough force to overwhelm every single one of them in the three caverns—at the same time.

Your troops can tell the Snakes from the Jaguars by the way they're dressed. We'll have the big-shots from the Cortes Syndicate, the Aztec, the Snakes and all the drugs. It'll break the back of the Syndicate. All we gotta do is lay low until the moon is overhead."

⊙ The Cortes drug cartel was headquartered in Mexico City, Mexico. The final push to bring organized Caribbean control of drugs, alcohol, prostitution, illegal arms and ransom is nearing completion. A week-long meeting of the eleven mobsters who control each of those five crime syndicates were in attendance. The concluding business was flying in separate planes and meeting at a bar named *The Bahamas Beauty*, in the town of Ocho Rios, Jamaica. Here they picked up Benito, the crime boss of the Jamaican branch of the Cortes Syndicate. They are at present, all twelve aboard a private, luxury airliner flying between Jamaica and Belize City, Belize.

Juan Cortes, mastermind in organizing the new Caribbean Crime Syndicate, was talking with his foremost captain, Benito Gomez, on the plane to Belize.

"So everything's arranged? I don't want any slip-ups. I've got 'em all lined up to put the organization into operation."

"No problems, Boss. The Aztec has it all set-up. We'll all board a big helicopter that's waiting at the Belize airport and go straight to the temple warehouse. I'm tellin ya Boss, it's gonna be a sweet deal. Wait til you see the stash of drugs we already got stockpiled."

"Yeah, Benito. I thought that Aztec Indian was crazy in the head when he came to me with this deal for a warehouse in the jungle. We still have to work out the logistics for distribution from there to the public."

"Be sure and tell these bozos", he nodded his head toward the syndicate passengers on the plane, "not to talk to the Indians. They're to remain detached because to the Indians they're gods possessed with magical powers. They'll each have a Mayan mask to wear and for no reason should they take it off until we leave the jungle."

"I'll tell 'em again. I'm having 'em leave their heat on the chopper. I don't trust them not to start somethin' because they think the Indians are stupid."

Benito stared at Cortes. "That Aztec is sure as hell not stupid, Boss. In fact that crazy bastard is sly as a fox. I recommend you keep him in the jungle where he can only mess with the Mayans.

"I plan to. I know you got him that stupid airplane he was so adamant about having? The damn thing was a deal breaker. How did you get it to him in the jungle?"

"Yeah, Boss. I had Kojo take care of it after you tipped me off it was in Jamaica. He's one big Haitian. Seven feet tall and almost crazy as the Aztec. He took steps to grab it and get it to him in the jungle."

"How is that black son-of-a-bitch doing? Causing any trouble?"

"He's alright as long as he gets his rum and a woman now and then."

"Make sure his doings does not come back on you."

"Yeah. I have that situation isolated. I've often wondered who messed him up so bad when he first came to us. Must'a been one tough bastard."

"Trust me, Benito, he is. His name is Barkow and I had his woman kidnapped by a gang I know in Tucson, because I heard he was flying to Belize. I didn't want him around our set-up."

"Where'd you hear that from?"

"I'd put a mole on the inside of Precision Trust who owned that Lancair and had him keeping tabs on its flight schedule. He picked up the info about Barkow and passed it on to me. You know Benito, I had that plane picked out for us to grab for the Aztec."

"Good deal, Boss. You always take precautions."

"Not so good, Benito. The son-of-a-bitch got off the damn plane when he heard we had his woman. Scared the living shit outa Scotty, the gang boss. Carved the letter 'C' in his cheek and said that stood for commitment. Totally ruined him to be any use to us. Last I heard Barkow was coming this way."

"Not a problem, Boss. We got this deal sewed up as tight as a bull's ass in fly-time."

The cabin speaker blared into life: "This is the Captain speaking. All passengers fasten seat belts. We will be landing at Belize International within ten minutes."

They set down without incident. The group wore light weight clothing and stepped from the plane to a wheeled disembarking stairway.

Walking through the tropical humidity and overbearing heat they quickly broke out in sweat as they trailed across the sunbaked asphalt to an airport bus which took them to waiting limousines in the airport parking lot. From there to a private resort where they would spend the time until the moon was rising, two hours before dawn. The final leg of their journey would be to fly in a helicopter to the Aztec's gala event, held in the jungle as a fitting finish to the creation of a Caribbean world-wide powerhouse of crime.

CHAPTER NINETEEN

THE CORTES CRIME Syndicate departed on time and flew through darkness until landing in the jungle; the only landing lights being on a cleared rectangle of jungle with a small bonfire at each corner.

Before debarking the copter, Cortes spoke to his cohorts in a very serious tone:

"Okay you men, listen up. During the time you are off this helicopter I want you to wear your Mayan mask at all times. You'll leave your heat here. Just leave it in the seat you're setting in."

"Bullshit!" exclaimed one of the gangsters. "I ain't leavin' my gun in no damn seat."

"If you're so much in love with the damn thing," Cortes shouted, "you can stay on the fucking ship 'til we come back"

"Well, dammit Boss, I don't feel good about bein' without it."

"Then stay here."

He grumbled to himself but did not speak aloud again.

"During the show, it's very important you wear the mask at all times. You'll each be handed a lightweight disguise, when you debark. It will depict an ancient Mayan god. These are savage tribesmen and probably will be stoned on drugs, but, I guarantee this show will be something that none of you will ever forget."

Gathered in a group, outside the helicopter, they snickered and poked fun at each other as they looked at each others mysterious and abhorrent masks being worn. All gaiety ceased when the repulsive features of the Aztec priest materialized in the glow of firelight. On either side, one step back, stood a Snake Warrior holding a tall lance, tipped with a narrow, razor-sharp, obsidian spear-point. A loin cloth made of snake skin along with a cloak-like affair made of the first three feet of a skinned boa, including the head, which made a mask-like headdress. The warrior's glittering eyes looked through the eye-openings of the snake-head skin. Above the left knee, encircling the leg, was a rattlesnake band, still holding the rattles, which chink-chinked with each left step. The entire body was painted in black snake skin patterns.

The priest's hideous face, painted to produce horror, stared from exceedingly bright eyes set in dark, russet colored skin with small, black painted jaguar spots all over the face. Long black hair tied up in a topknot fell down his back on a jaguar skin draped across his shoulders. White fangs were painted from his upper lip to chin and long, black hair hung around his face falling to his shoulders. A black and coral snake-skin band circled his throat. His arms and torso were painted with large Jaguar spots, as were his legs. He wore a loin cloth of Jaguar skin and a pair of shoulder boards covered with black and white ocelot fur.

"Come," he commanded and strode away, holding a burning torch, through the darkness. Cortes, Benito and the rest, wearing Mayan-god disguises, fell into single file behind him and the two Snake Warriors brought up the rear. They walked a small distance, unaware that from high in the branches of a tree on the outskirts of the cleared landing site, Barkow and Con watched their progress toward the low, open mouth of the cave.

As soon as the group was gone from sight of the landed helicopter, the pilot and his co-pilot exited the craft and walked over to the edge of the clearing where they sat on rolled up jungle-camo webbing, used to conceal the clearing from passing aircraft. One shook out a cigarette from the pack and lighted it. The other relaxed with his back against a tree trunk, looking up at the full moon almost directly overhead.

Noiselessly, Barkow and Con slipped down from their tree across the clearing. They moved silently and effortlessly as moon shadows, around the perimeter of the clearing until they were directly behind the two man crew.

The Mayan-masked mobsters were following the Aztec through the low mouth of the cavern with the two warriors bringing up the rear The camp sites had been cleared from a central area and long, low tables constructed in preparation for the feast to follow.

Set in rows and placed on the tables were hundreds of banana leaf place settings with drinking vessels made from sections of bamboo. Large containers of fermented fruit juice, with gourd ladles, were scattered here and there upon the tables. Hollow sections, split apart, of a tropical tree trunk, were piled to overflowing with corncakes. Bonfires lighted the camp giving a warm, festive look.

As the masked racketeers followed the Aztec between the rows of tables, they saw the double-doors of *The Room of the Lost* had been thrown open. Five naked men, painted blue, were dragging out bamboo cages and forcing the nude occupants to crawl from their now open enclosures. The blue men had sharp pointed sticks which they used to jab the captives, prodding them to hurry their exit from the cage. Some, blinded by the torchlight, could not stand and they were cruelly jabbed with the prodding sticks that had been dipped in a substance that made each jab sting like putting salt on a wound. Those that could not unbend, had their joints forcefully pulled back and forth by blue hands and were repeatedly beaten and poked with the sticks or urged by other methods to stand in line. One man in particular was pleading and crying out in pain. He could neither rise nor stand. They would put him on his feet only to have him fall, whimpering, to the ground. Finally one of the blue men took a burning brand from a fire and began scorching the skin of the screaming captive until Gary Appleton forced himself to stand upright.

The masked men of the Cortes Syndicate nudged one another and pointed at the captives as they were tied at the neck to long poles. There were four peeled poles with seven notches cut at intervals along the length of each. A captive's neck was tied against a notch so they could not move from their position along the pole where it rested upon their shoulder. The Aztec priest later led the first pole of seven naked captives through his living quarters and out into the sacred passage that ran between his rooms and the now unblocked exit close to the wye junction.

"Who are those people in the cages we passed?" One of the gang members called out.

"They are being prepared for your pleasure." The Aztec said.

"Come," he commanded as he strode out of the Indian camp area and into the tunnel leading to the *Temple of the Snake,* holding the torch high. The disguised leaders of the Cortes Crime Syndicate trailed in his wake followed by the two Snake Warriors. After a short way they turned off the tunnel into a storage room filled with packaged drugs.

"This just beginning," the Aztec said. "Soon there be many storerooms filled for syndicate use."

He led them to a second storeroom, dimly lighted by a few oil lamps. A putrid odor hung in the air around a long row of large pots half-filled with water. The face-concealed men wandered around, looking at the pots, the tables and assorted flint knives and tools.

A group of naked Mayans, appeared to be painted black, stood along one wall. In good light it would have been noticed their hair was matted with dried blood. Their bodies stank of death. Their hands and arms were heavily coated with layers of blackish, dried blood. These were those who never washed and would prepare the flesh of twenty-eight to be sacrificed, for the feast to follow.

At the back of the room, dug into the wall, were shelves, faintly visible in the flickering flames of the lamps. One man ventured closer to the crude, dirt shelves and with a loud curse, expressed his disgust as he hurried back to his companions.

"No wonder it stinks in here." He bellowed. "They've got some god-damned rotting heads back there."

"You sure about that?" Said another.

"Hell yes, I'm sure. I know what a fucking human head looks like."

"Come!" Shouted the Aztec priest and strode out of the room. The two Snake Warriors quickly rounded up the Mayan-masked men and herded them from the room. They walked down the tunnel and into the temple. They were acutely aware of the sound of a soft, thudding drum beating a slow, mind numbing rhythm. The Aztec, leading the group, forced his way through the slow-moving, ghostly forms of befuddled Indians, swaying to the drumbeat, in a haphazard, drugged cadence. The temple was lighted by sputtering oil lamps. Oil rendered out of fat, taken from sacrificed victims. A small packet was pushed into the hand of each visitor as they were seated in a row of high chairs facing the near-vertical temple stairs, on the right side of the packed crowd, their voices now building into a blood lust. They gave fourth loud and mysterious lamentations and howling or wailing demanding the soon to be sacrificed victims. From the temple floor before the seated syndicate men, rose the sweet, stench of rotting roses and congealed human blood.

"What the hell is this?" Said one visitor as he showed his little paper packet to the man seated next to him.

"It's cocaine ya dumb shit. Taste it."

"Jesus, this is the real stuff. It's uncut."

CHAPTER TWENTY

THE PILOT AND co-pilot of the helicopter never heard a sound as Barkow and Con, each took a man to a state of unconsciousness. They carried them into the now landed whirlybird which they had flown in. There, bound together, back to back, in such a way, they could neither move about nor see each other. Next they reset the bonfires so they outlined a square of cleared space behind the landed copter.

Con called in the incoming chopper with the first group of twenty commandos who rappelled from the hovering aircraft, followed by the second ship and so on until all five had offloaded one hundred men in full combat gear. The operation had been flawlessly planned and executed. Every commando had been briefed as to how it would take place. The jungle troops, upon landing, formed into five waves of twenty men.

The first wave, without a sound, entered the cave at the exact moment the last pole of prisoners followed by two Snake Warriors, exited into the Aztec's rooms. Eventually their route, as with the captives ahead of them, would take them through the secret tunnel leading from the Aztec living quarters to the back entrance of the temple.

When that first wave was inside, to a depth of ten feet, the second wave came in to integrate with them, increasing the proportions of that wave to forty men covering the entire width of the camp. Twenty-eight empty bamboo captive cages were scattered about the entrance to the room of the lost. They moved forward looking under the tables and into anyplace a person could hide. At one end they pulled apart the palm fronds covering the stolen

Lancair and looked inside. They quietly ransacked the Snake Warriors quarters, finding drugs but no people. In the Room of the Lost, they found only an ungodly stench. The Aztec's rooms rewarded them with an automatic rifle, a couple of pistols and some grenades, which were removed and placed under guard.

The third wave of twenty commandos, led by Barkow, formed into a double file outside, then entered the cavern. They dog-trotted to the tunnel with storerooms that connected to the sanctuary. As they entered, Barkow sent the first four men into the storeroom on the left and the next four into the one on the right. Moving on he did the same with the next two rooms. Now left with only four men he approached the next room. The men in the first room found no-one there and quickly came out to form up behind those with Barkow. The men from the second room, also found no-one and immediately fell-in with Barkow's group. They cleared each storeroom in the same fashion. Anyone found was at once secured with plastic tie-ties and gagged, then left in that storeroom. The room with pots of water and the shelved, severed heads contained twelve men. They were taken so quickly, silenced and secured that no sound was heard in the tunnel proper.

Fourth wave, led by Con, was hand-picked for size and ability. They were small men with holstered automatics beneath their left armpits. Each had belted trench knives and were equipped with powerful flashlights. They moved quickly in single file through the jungle from the cave mouth to the whirlpool then around it to the root-bound entrance into the River Cavern. They left two men as a rear guard and the rest gathered just inside.

They spread into a line covering the width of the cave from river to back wall and advanced, leaving two men at a stela which stood before the enhanced snake mouth entrance of the tunnel leading to the wye junction. They continued onward, not stopping until they came to the caves end-wall where the river went underground. They had found no-one and re-formed at the tunnels entrance by the stela. Con scouted ahead through the length of the tunnel and found two Warriors supposedly guarding the tunnel, but in truth were watching the process at the junction.

Captives were now, one at a time, being released from their pole and prodded into the opening behind the carved serpent with jade eyes. The Aztec climbed up first followed by a warrior and five naked, blue-painted men. With vicious jabs from pointed prod-sticks, warriors forced the first released captive to follow the last blue man up the steep climb of stone stairs to the altar platform, then the second, the third and so on.

The fifth and last wave of twenty commandos, with caution and stealth, as if following a group of man-eating jaguars, now silently trailed in the darkness, behind the two Snake Warriors bringing up the rear of the twenty-eight pole-bound captives.

On the platform at the top of the inner stairway, the Aztec, one Snake warrior and five blue-painted holders were hidden from view of the Mayan people below on the floor, including the twelve white men seated in the front row at the foot of the temple stairway, wearing Mayan masks.

In the small hut-like building high upon the altar platform, located over the top of the near-vertical back stairway guarded by a Warrior, cringed the first captive, shaking with fear.

On the platform in front of the of the two Mayan god images, charcoal burned cherry-red in pit depressions built into the tiled floor, creating that bizarre glow illuminating the two effigies. Somewhere a muffled drum beat a slow, hypnotic pulse. Two blue holders came from the building and a substance was pushed onto the coals before both effigies, creating a huge, billowing, cloud of olive colored smoke, engulfing the entire platform. The Aztec slipped unseen through the murk, consisting of minute particles suspended in a gas, to stand before the altar. As the haze dispersed the hideous presence of that sacrificial priest materialized before the tribe gathered below. He stood arms raised and feet apart.

His appearance caused an eerie silence from the natives,

most of whom were under the influence of drugs. When the Aztec brought his arms down and feet together the drumbeat stopped. He held the sacrificial knife handle with both hands against his chest, blade pointing to his chin.

In the unearthly silence he began a low, slow chant; ah.... ne....oh....oh—ah...ne...oh...oh. Here and there the spaced out crowd below, began to pick up the chant. Others joined as the refrain grew louder and faster. The syllables came more rapidly as the crazed Indians began connecting them together, screaming a single word, ahneeohcho, ahneeohcho!

Con crept back to his group, then brought them silently through the tunnel and close to the guards watching the captives, one at a time, being untied from their pole and sent forth following the one before him. The last two poles of bound captives were now in the tunnel leading from the Aztec's rooms to the wye junction and the back stairs to the sacrificing platform. The line slowly moved forward until it stopped, backed up to a point where the almost perpendicular, back stone steps leading up to the interior of the hut-like structure atop the temple's high platform was clogged with intended victims of sacrifice. The final pole, with seven captives attached, waited at the end of the line. The commandos following the line of captives waited in the darkness behind the final pole of captives waiting in line.

All was ready for the moment of rescue to take place. Con and the fourth wave were grouped in the tunnel coming from the river in the first cavern to the wye junction. Barkow and the third wave were grouped in the tunnel from camp area to the Mayan shrine. The fifth wave stood waiting at the exit of the tunnel from the Aztec's quarters to the wye junction. The first and second wave covered the entrance to the mouth of the Residence Cavern and the Jaguar camp area, including the captive holding room of the lost, plus the Aztec and Snake Warrior's living quarters.

Each wave had a commander and a radio man keeping them in contact with each other. At a given password they would all move forward and begin taking control of each and every Indian in the complex. Resistance would be met with absolute force to the death if required. The password was, *Takedown*. Each radio man stood by his commander.

The supreme commander, Major Bohannan, spoke into his mike with a strong, clear voice. "Takedown! Takedown! All Troops execute Takedown." The great hand of law, order and justice closed upon the entire Jaguar Tribe and Snake Warriors like a giant fist.

Con and his twenty men overpowered the two guards and charged the Snakes gathered around the final pole of captives. Ten Commandos continued on past, as five of them blocked the right and five the left hand tunnels to the sanctuary; making them escape-proof—into or out of the sanctuary.

Twenty men of the fifth-wave charged out of the tunnel connecting the Aztec's rooms to the wye. Five to left and five to right reinforcing the troopers blocking the two tunnels in preparation of rushing the temple floor to start herding all the Indians together in the temple. The other ten charged into the troopers and Snakes engaged around the coiled serpent sculpture at the back entrance to the killing platform. The drug crazed Snake Warriors fought like demons but were swiftly killed, maimed or taken prisoner. They were forced face-down and tied with their wrists strapped to their ankles.

The captives going up the stone stairway were rescued, one by one, helped back down and grouped with the others. The last captive was replaced by a Jungle Trooper, who killed the single Snake Warrior in the hut-like building. The steep staircase was soon clogged with the following jungle troops. They rushed from the top onto the sacrificial platform as the terrified, naked blue men, seeing the commandos materializing in the swirling remains of foggy smoke, started down the steep staircase to the inner floor, with Troopers right behind them. Down the stairs they flooded into a now milling Jaguar Tribe below. In perfect concert Barkow and his men poured out of the tunnel of storerooms and Con's men surged from both entrances on either side of the inner stairway. The Aztec, assessing the situation, had immediately gone to one side of the stairway and was carefully making his way down the high, steep steps while rubbing off and smearing the spots painted on his body. He ripped off the Jaguar skin from his shoulders and discarded it while he fought his way into the crowd, hoping to become concealed as one of the Jaguar tribe members.

Together, Barkow and thirty-five troopers stormed from the tunnel of storerooms across the backside of the crowd stringing out to put a connected ring of Jungle Troopers around the crowd. The remaining five blocked the tunnel so none could escape out that way. Some Snake Warriors tried to put up a defense but were soon killed or subdued, forced face-down and hogtied where they fell. Those that mingled into the crowd were easily ferreted out because their apparel identified them at once. The men of the Cortes Syndicate had discarded their masks as they split up trying to escape. When captured they were also thrown face-down on the bloody floor near their raised seats and secured, as were the others. Because of their leader's demands, they'd left their weapons in the helicopter seats and had no way to create problems.

In the commotion, the Aztec staggered, dragging one leg and bent over like a cripple, into the Jaguar tribesmen. He was physically forcing his way through the Mayans milling around on the floor as he worked his way toward Chaac's forbidden room. Benito, seeing his boss Juan Cortes clubbed senseless also noticed the Aztec priest fighting his way through the crowd toward the temple wall. The Commandos were searching out the Snakes in the melee and securing them. Some people of the Jaguar Tribe who could still function, started to abuse the bound Snake Warriors. They spit on them, kicked them and yanked their hair. Some snatched away their rattlesnake rattles for souvenirs. The Priest broke free and dashed into Chaac's sacred room with Benito darting in behind him. In the darkened dead end of the room the Priest pushed on a certain rock in the rear wall's corner and a three foot section of wall turned sideways on center mounted pins top and bottom. The Priest slipped through and as he tried to push the section back into place, Benito fought his way through also.

The raid had gone as planned. In the short time of thirty minutes the troopers had everything in order and began the processing phase. Each captive had been given a fits-all cotton gown to cover their nakedness and separated from the Mayans. Tribe members were herded into the camp area and sat at the tables, after the fermented juice had been dumped out.

The Aztec or Benito were never found. It was decided they had somehow concealed themselves somewhere inside the caverns and possibly had managed to slip away into the jungle. The Snakes were brought out and without ceremony, bound as were the others and placed into *The Room of the Lost*, to enjoy the stench and darkness.

Con found the corncake woman sitting with two deaf boys.

"Greetings, Mother." He spoke in a quiet voice. "Are you alright?"

"Yes, my Son. All is well. This old woman is happy for you."

"Mother, I will provide you with a helicopter ride to Belize City if you wish to return to civilization."

"I have no one to go to, Conchaco. No one wants a useless old woman."

"I know a group of elderly Mayan people who live on the outskirts of the city and would welcome you among them."

"I cannot leave the boys, Conchaco. They have no one and would starve to death. Thank you, but I must stay with them."

Conchaco smiled. "They would also be welcomed. I have told these old people you make the best corncakes in all of Belize."

"Do you mean I could take the deaf boys with me?"

"Oh yes, Mother. But you may not be able to sleep because of the noise. Their camp is by a beautiful waterfall and is so noisy. Oh, and the birds at sunrise make so many different calls and whistles. I am sure you would not like that."

"Conchaco. Shame on you, teasing an old woman like this."

Con slowly shook his head. "Worst of all, Mother, those old men would always be wanting you to dance with them and feed them corncakes."

Her wrinkled old face broke into a constellation of smiles as she came to him with open arms. He held her in his arms and whispered in her ear. "Conchaco loves you, Mother. Everything will be alright."

Barkow found Roni and Appleton with the other captives who were being treated for their wounds. He knelt beside her.

"Hi Veronica, remember me?"

"Barkow, thank God you saved us from those hideous vultures. I'm still shaking from fright. Can you get some medical help for Gary? He's critically burned and I think out of his mind from fear."

Barkow called a medic over and asked him to look at Appleton, who, shaking, was huddled in a fetal position. The medic had a problem examining him because he could not get him to open up.

"I think he has some sort of a psychiatric disorder." The medic said and called two men with a stretcher. They carried Appleton away.

"Are you physically unharmed, Roni?"

"I think so. I'm just sore from being cramped in that cage."

"If you want to call in your story I suggest you do it right away because the word will get out as soon as the captives are in a hospital. You will be sent out on the first helicopter. I can have someone meet you and arrange for whatever you need."

"Yes. Thank God, Barkow. That would be wonderful. How will I know who it is.?"

"It's gonna be that same Policeman you asked for help before you got yourself kidnapped. If I can reach him. If not, I will get someone, so don't worry about it. The code word will be "Blue Note. They will also bring you pen, paper and clipboard with some better clothes. You can use a Police unit if you want to write the story on computer. Just be thinking about how to set up your story."

"Thank you so much. How will I contact you when you get back to the city?"

"Call me at the same hotel. Leave a message if I'm not there. I have your laptop in a safe place and you can get it when I get back."

Veronica threw her arms around Barkow and pressed herself against him. He could feel her unbound breasts through the cotton gown pressed against his chest.

"I knew you would come." She said. "Somehow I knew you would be the one to rescue me. I kept telling myself, 'Barkow will be here, he will, I know he will'.

At that moment a medic came up and said; "Time to go Miss. The bird is warming up for takeoff. Are you able to walk or do you need a stretcher?"

"I can walk as long as we go slowly. Goodbye, Barkow. I'll see you back in Belize city."

"Bye, Roni. See you then. Remember to get your copy in as soon as you land."

Barkow watched the helicopter lift off, orient itself to the course, drop its nose and quickly fade into the darkness. He hunted up Con and together they went to the Lancair. The palm fronds had been removed by the troopers who'd searched for anyone that may be hiding when they came through.

"Yup. This is the missing plane alright. I can call Great Metro and they'll take it from here. Wonder why that Aztec wanted it."

"Him want be big-shot gangster."

"My one regret is that son-of-a-bitch slipped away in the confusion."

"Him live two haab' in jungle—alone. Him plenty smart fella."

"I've heard that word before. What's a haab'?"

"Maya calendar. Same-same one year. Haab' have 18 month, 20 day each and 1 month 5 day.

"I heard ancient Mayan's had time and calendars and religion all intermixed."

"That is true, Boss. I want to check something out. You wanna come with me?"

"Sure. Where are we headed?"

"Boss Man follow."

The two friends worked their way down by the whirlpool and Con carefully studied the ground along the riverbank.

"What you looking for, Con?"

"Boss remember putting sensor on canoe?"

"Sure Con, but we don't need to find it.."

"Con wants to see that canoe"

A while later they came upon several canoes pulled upon the bank. They searched for the canoe with the sensor but it appeared to be missing.

"Does Boss still have tracking GPS device?"

"Yes. It's in my backpack back at the mouth to the tribal cavemouth."

They hurried back and found the backpack and with the GPS unit and turned it on.

"My God!" Barkow gasped. "Look at that, Con."

The blinking dot on the screen showed the canoe was steadily traveling back up the river away from the whirlpool. Barkow gave the tracking device to Major Bohannan who at once ordered out a search party. Six men would start upriver from the whirlpool and six would leap-frog ahead and start downriver from the lagoon as soon as the motorized shallow riverboats could be flown in.

Barkow and Con boarded the last helicopter, after the captives and the Cortes Syndicate gang were flown away. The Jaguar Tribe was being processed along with the Snake Warriors and would remain at the temple under guard until a location and charges were decided on.

CHAPTER TWENTY-ONE

THE PLANTATION LAY at the edge of vast jungle wetlands that covered a great share of northeast Belize. Barkow was following the directions Con had given him to find his home. He drove along a dirt lane of long curves that swept through shady, green forest of broad leafed trees, thickets of black bamboo and the ever present tree ferns. Here and there rays of sunshine speared through the canopy of foliage to create splotches of brightness at ground level.

He rounded a broad curve and as the road straightened out, rolled beneath an entrance. Two upright logs planted, one at each side of the lane with another, notched and placed across their tops. From rusted chains, a huge, wooden slab hung crossways above the road. The words 'Plantation Maya' were carved deeply into its width. A short way forward he drove into a cleared area centered by a large two story house with palm thatched roof. A number of cars, pickups, ATVs and vans were haphazardly parked on the vastness of a grassy meadow that surrounded the house. Groups of people were scattered around utilizing some picnic tables. Beyond the tables, safely away from the house, stood a huge iron barbecue with two whole pigs turning on a spit above the coals. Their golden brown texture glistened with basting juices as they slowly rotated in the heated air.

Barkow parked his rental and made his way toward the barbeque pit. As he approached he saw Veronica Lowen cutting across the grass to meet him. Her doe-brown hair, short in back but lengthened out on top, swooped across her forehead, giving her an impish look. As she approached, the sleeveless silk blouse draped around her torso looked highly sensual in the way it emphasized her breasts. Her hips, enclosed in a wraparound skirt, rolled with every step showing a bare leg, halfway up the thigh, as she walked directly toward him until they stopped before each other.

"Hello, Barkow. I'm so glad you came. I looked forward to seeing you." She spoke in a throaty purr, reminiscent of cream & warmed whiskey. His gray eyes glittered and in that brief moment, she couldn't tell if desire or anger was at the source. That gleam, instantly replaced by a friendly look as taut lips relaxed into a smile; he wrapped his arms around her in a brotherly hug.

"Wouldn't miss it for the world," he said as he broke from the hug and taking her hand they began to walk. "Have you turned in your story?"

"Oh, yes. I wrote it in my mind on the flight to town and faxed it in as soon as I had it on paper." She flicked a glance at him from the corner of her eye as they walked through the grass.

"The editor called back and congratulated me. He wants all the follow-up copy I can get."

"Great." Barkow said. "Looks like you got your scoop."

"Thanks to you and I want to repay your kindness in any way I can." She dropped his hand and stopped, hastily turning to face him. It took him by surprise, causing him to collide with her, again aware of her breasts pushing firmly against him. "Oh, Barkow, I'm sorry." She stammered, stepping back. "I didn't mean to cause a collision and I apologize."

"Not necessary," he murmured. "I'm glad I could be of help. How is Appleton doing, have you heard?"

"I think his mind is gone. The paper has flown him to a hospital in San Fran. When would be a good time to meet and get my laptop back?"

"Anytime in the next day or two. I'm at the same hotel. I hope to be leaving for Phoenix soon as I wrap up a few final details."

She smiled, thin and razor sharp. "I'll give a call before I come over."

"Good." He said. At that moment the squeaky, rusty-pump call of Bluebird sounded across the field, thin as crystal in the afternoon air. "That's my call. Gotta go round up Con and see what he wants. Take care of yourself, Roni, and good luck on the paper."

"Sure, Barkow. Will do, see you later." She broke off and walked away in a different direction, head down, making plans.

Barkow angled across the turf towards the barbecue pit where a man was dipping basting juice from a metal bucket onto the turning meat.

"Hi. That smells awfully good," Barkow said to the man. "Is Con around?"

"Thank you. It's about ready to eat, just as soon as they bring out the rest of the food," he said. "Conchaco is in the house, I think."

"Okay, thanks. I'll check over there." Barkow said and started toward the house, threading his way through long tables upon which women were placing various dishes of food. The food-tables were surrounded by many picnic tables with built-in seats. He mounted the steps to a screened veranda that completely encircled the house. People were everywhere, strolling about the grass, standing in groups talking and laughing.

He walked up the steps and entered the veranda where more people were sitting on chesterfields, sofas and settees. Others were meandering about through the many clusters of individuals who stood talking, telling jokes and chuckling. Most folks seemed to have a drink in their hand. It was party time on a grand scale.

Barkow stopped a man who was carrying a tray of drinks through the press of people and asked for some help.

"Pardon me, pal. Can you tell me where I can find Con?"

"He was on the south wall by the bar a while ago."

"Thank you. Which way is the south wall?"

"Ah, I see you're new here. Just keep going the way I came from and turn the corner. You will find the Bar about the center of the veranda."

"Okay. Thanks a lot."

"No problem. Have a drink." He lowered the tray and held it before Barkow.

"I'm Chico. Welcome to the Plantation. Conchaco is on the move, so you may have to keep looking for a while, but you will eventually catch up with him."

"Thanks Chico. I'm Barkow," he said as he took the offered drink. At that moment the loud racket of horns, drums, guitars and bells began blaring just outside the screened veranda on the grass. It seemed to be a signal for people to dance because suddenly it appeared everyone was swaying in fluctuation with rumba moves. Chico laughed and moved on with a cha-cha step making his way through the dancers.

Barkow tasted his tropical drink of rum and fruit juice, then began to work his way to and around the corner where he soon found the bar, doing a big business with a crowd packed around it. It was recessed into the wall of the house with just the stand-up bar jutting out from the side of the wall with the typical brass foot rail below. Barkow noticed there were several large, clear glass-cylinders along the bar. They were now about half full of money. A half dozen bartenders were making drinks for the customers and payment was whatever you wanted to put in the cylinders.

Barkow edged his way to the bar and dropped a twenty in the cylinder.

"Has Conchaco been here lately?" He asked.

"He was here a while ago," said the barman, "I think he left when the dancing started. Try the dance floor. What do you want to drink?"

"I'm good. Thanks for the info." Barkow proceeded to make his way out of the crowd at the bar and continue around the veranda. As the racket of musical instruments fell into a mellow rumba beat, he rounded the next corner and saw a dance floor, situated a few yards from the veranda steps to the lawn. It seemed to be made of patterned tiles set into a concrete slab.

Perhaps a dozen couples were swaying to the beat of the music. He picked out Con dancing with an elderly woman in a bright red and yellow dress. He remained on the veranda, taking a seat in a vacant porch swing and sipped his drink as he watched the dancers.

"Well, hello again stranger." Roni said as she sat down beside him in the swing. "Did you find your friend?" He felt the heat of her thigh pressing against his own.

"Hi, Roni. Yeah, he's on the dance floor. I'm waiting for him to finish up."

"It's shaping up to be a wild party." She spoke as she looked askance at him with lidded eyes across the rim of her glass, then gently tipped it to her lips and took a slow drink while she studied him.

Something, drifting on a trace of memory, tugged at his mind. Barkow lifted his glass and swallowed, letting the rum's heat settle in his belly and spread, as obvious certainties ran rampant through his thoughts. *She's definitely on the make and it's impossible for me not to be attracted to her sexually. It's like the call from a ghost of expensive perfume. Something about the reckless way she pushes herself at me is shouting beware…danger." It's a foregone conclusion she'd be uninhibited as a feral cat in the bedroom. A man could break self-promises for what she's offering.*

He stood up and turned toward her. With feet spread slightly apart, he looked down upon Veronica, analyzing the guarded shadows in her eyes, then allowed his gaze to slide down, to a point between her exposed breasts. She leaned slightly forward and turned her face up, first letting her eyes reveal an innocent stare, then make a conversion to one of erotic lust.

Barkow's face was completely expressionless, save for whatever burned, far back in the depths of those steel-gray eyes that glittered for the moment, but whether with pleasure or rage, she couldn't be sure. He beheld her in one praising look, turned on his heel and strode away.

Apparently he's not ready yet, she thought, *but wait 'til I pick up*

*my laptop. I've never yet missed getting the man I wanted to have...
and I intend to have that one.*

Barkow went back to the bar and ordered bourbon neat. He strolled into the house interior and joined a group of people around a beautiful young woman, of Mayan descent, playing the piano. She was playing some old torch songs of the 40s. When she finished, he leaned across the piano and dropped a twenty in the brandy snifter tip jar and said, "Do you happen to know 'Chains of Love'?"

"Of course. I will be happy to play it for you, Mr. Barkow."

"Cut the Mr. and just call me Barkow. Do I know you?"

As she began playing a soft introduction to the song she murmured, "I recognized your voice at once."

"From where, may I ask?"

"From when you called for the Jungle Man," she smiled. "I'm Lila, Conchaco's daughter."

"That explains it. Nice to meet you Lila. You play as lovely as you look." Barkow smiled and raised his glass in a silent toast to her as she broke into the main theme of the song. The music brought a deep longing for Laura and he wished she were with him. As the song came to an end, someone touched his shoulder and he turned to find Conchaco beside him.

They shook hands and each put his free arm around the other in a gesture of friendship.

"Have you met my daughter, the piano player?" Con said.

"Yes, she introduced herself to me. She's a lovely girl and plays the piano very well."

"Thank you, Boss Man." Con spoke with a grin. "She takes after her mother."

"Is that who you were dancing with a while ago?"

"No. That was the corncake lady who helped us save the captives in the temple."

"Ah, yes. You told me she would be coming to Belize City."

"She has moved into The Village here on the Plantation. She takes care of the two deaf boys who cannot speak."

"That's one of the best things that came out of the mess in the temple. Has the Aztec been located yet?"

"No. The man's slippery as a snake. He can survive in the jungle, but I have a feeling he'll try to get to Jamaica or go into Guatemala. I don't think he will go to Mexico because he's wanted there by the Police as well as here, in Belize."

"Con. You've lost your accent. What happened to my Jungle Man?"

"When I play the role of a jungle guide, I find it is better to simply act as though I am just that and only that." He smiled. "I hope you'll forgive me."

"Consider it done," Barkow said. "I have a little gift for you in my car. I would like to present it to you sometime today."

"Of course. Today I will give a talk to the folks gathered here. You can do your thing at that time. It will take place after we eat."

"Great. By the way, who takes care of *The Village* we'd talked about?"

"Oh. That's something I do for the old folks. It is very nice for those who have no place else to go."

"How many are living there?"

"Ninety-two at present."

"It must be very expensive to operate with living quarters and meals provided."

"Not really. They grow much of their own food and make a lot of things for the tourist trade."

"It's very generous of you,"

"Let's eat some barbeque." Con said. The two friends went out and loaded up plates of food and found a place at one of the tables. Lila and her mother joined them as well as an assortment of aunts, uncles, and various other relatives. Barkow was formally introduced to each one and also made into an honorary family member. After they finished the two hour meal, a small stage was set up with a microphone. Con gave a short speech in which he thanked everyone for coming. He introduced both the

Corncake woman and Barkow as new members of his family and then called Barkow up to the mike.

"Attention my friends and my family. I have introduced this man to you as my brother and a family friend. I now wish to present to him a gift for being my friend." He brought forth the revolver and gun-belt Barkow had used during their trips into the jungle. "I took the liberty of having this Dan Wesson .357 Magnum revolver, engraved. It reads: *To Boss Man Barkow from Conchaco. Friends forever.* It is designed and built to be the most accurate, rugged and versatile revolver on the market and I am proud to give it to my friend, Barkow."

A huge cheer went up and Barkow took the mike from Con. "My Brother Conchaco has given me one of the finest weapons a man can own. I shall cherish it for the balance of my life and if I am blessed with children, it shall become a family heirloom to be passed down for generations. I regret I can only offer him a small token in return." He brought forth a small box and handed it to Con.

Con opened the box and drew forth the Bowie knife Barkow had worn during his jungle trips. He pulled it from the custom handmade leather sheaf that straps to the thigh and holding the crosshatched handle, held it up to the cheering crowd.

"It is also engraved on the blade, just below the handle," he spoke into the mike. "It reads: *To Con from Barkow, brothers of the heart, friends forever.*"

"Thank you, my Brother. I see we think the same way," Con said. "We both had engraving done on our gifts."

"And we both thought of the same thing." Barkow said.

"Wait, there is an envelope here also," Con drew an envelope from the box.

"No, Con. That is for private reading." Barkow said as Con was reading the inscription on the envelope.

"Nonsense," Con declared, looking at the envelope. "It is addressed to me. It says, *To Con – Read privately.*"

"Yes." Barkow exclaimed. You can look at it later."

Con tore open the envelope and drew forth a scribbled note attached to a check. His amplified voice boomed over the crowd. "It says: *'Here's a bit of help for The Village.'* And let's see, the check is signed by Barkow and…Oh my God! Oh my God, Barkow." He grabbed Barkow in a one armed bear hug and jumped up and down while shaking his hand "Thank you, Brother. Thank you for your generosity. My friends," he spoke in the mike. "Mr. Barkow has just given me a check for 100,000.00 dollars which he donates to *The Village.*" People cheered and whistled.

"That was meant to be given anonymously." Barkow muttered.

CHAPTER TWENTY-TWO

BARKOW DID NOT stay late. He drove back to his hotel in Belize City. In his room he found the phone message-light flashing. He punched the button and a recorded voice informed him a UPS container had been delivered to the hotel, for him. He asked them to send it up to his room. When it was brought up, he tipped the bell-boy and opened the package. It was a bottle of Blanton's, straight from the keg bourbon. A hand written note and a CD were also enclosed.

Barkow, my love,

Enjoy the bourbon and music.

I miss you terribly.

All my love,

Laura

Barkow filled a glass with ice and topped it off with the gift from Laura. He turned the lights low, slipped the Compact disk into a player and settled down to relax to the mellow sound of Laura playing '*The Chains of Love*'. In his mind's eye he could see her sitting at the piano playing with her beautiful eyes closed, the rich honey-gold hue of her hair made a perfect border, framing the face he'd learned to love. He could smell the memorable scent of gardenia on the note and his mind drifted back through time to where they'd first held each other close, dancing to this very song. For a while time slowed, dissolved and ceased to exist for Barkow, as he re-lived that dance in his mind.

The CD was set to repeat, the lights were low and the

bourbon was smooth as a whisper of silk. He used the satellite phone and called the Blue Note.

"Blue Note. This is Bobby, may I help you?"

'Hi Bobby, how goes the battle?"

"Hey, Boss. How're you doin'? When you comin' home?"

"With any luck I'll be on a plane tomorrow. How's business?"

"It's going great. Our client count is up. Sales are increasing and Laura is packin' 'em in. Did you know she cut a CD with Jackie?"

"Yeah, she sent one to me. Sounds great. Is Laura there now?"

"She's in her office on a break. You wanna talk to her?"

"Yeah, patch me through."

"Kay-kay. Hang one."

"Hello. May I help you?"

"If you were here you could help me a lot," he said.

"Barkow? Hi Babe, are you home yet?"

"Not yet, Laura, but probably tomorrow."

"Oh, Barkow. I miss you so much. Let me know when you get in so I can meet you at the airport."

"Not necessary. My car is in the long-term storage lot. I'll let you know the arrival time and meet you at the condo."

"That will be fantastic. God, I've been missing you so much. Do you think you can get here in early afternoon?"

"Maybe. I haven't called the airport yet, but I'll let you know as soon as I find out. By the way, I received your gift. It's great because I can't find it here to buy. I have your CD playing and like you, it's beautiful."

"Oh! I'm so happy. Please hurry home as quickly as you can. I can't wait to hold you again. How did your trip go? Is everything alright? I'm so excited just to hear your voice. I love you Barkow. I always have and always will. Please hurry home to me darling. Please come as…."

"Laura, Honey. Slow down. You're talking so fast I can't keep up." He laughed and then spoke in a serious, low voice. "I think too much of you to stay away very long. I need to call Harry at

Great-Metro and see if there are any last details. I think it's all finished up now, but need to check."

"Okay. Call me as soon as you have an arrival time tomorrow. I'm waiting on pins and needles, just for you. Stay safe and I love you always."

"I love you more than you know," he said. I'll call you tomorrow. Sleep well and goodbye until we meet again."

"Goodbye darling, until tomorrow."

He cut the connection and placed the satellite phone on the nightstand. He swallowed the last remains of his drink and put the empty glass beside the phone, then stretched out on the bed and let his mind wander. *Damn, I wish Laura was here with me. The more I think of her the more I want her. I'm probably in love with that woman. The quicker I can leave for home the happier I'll be. And when I get her alone…*Like an unexpected thunderbolt, the sudden, resounding clang of the room-phone interrupted his thoughts. Barkow let his mind forget thoughts of home and picked up the phone.

"Barkow."

"Hello, Barkow, Harry here."

"Hi, Harry. I was just getting ready to give you a call."

"I wanted to touch base and let you know Precision Thrust has a team on the way to pick up the Lancir."

"Good. They can get in touch with Sargent Conchaco of the Jungle Patrol. He can be helpful in steering them to the right people for removing the plane."

"Thanks. I'll pass that along."

"They're going to have a time getting it out of the cave and from there out of the jungle. It has no landing gear attached. Best way, may be to haul it out with a heavy duty helicopter."

"Yeah, gotcha. You can forget about it. Your job is finished and you can go home. You did great, Barkow, just as I knew you would."

"When I get home I'll fax you my report and a cover-sheet on the search details and expense account."

"Good. Thanks for dropping everything and doing this job for me. I appreciate it and next time we meet, I'll buy dinner. I hope it won't be long. How is your business venture going?"

"It's good. I have a great team running the show and they've become personal friends. Business has steady clientele growth. It will turn out to be an excellent investment."

"Glad to hear it. Let's keep in touch. See you when you're in New York or I get to Arizona and thanks again for the fine job you did."

"Your welcome, Harry. I'm glad I could help."

Barkow hung up the phone and fixed another Blanton's on ice as Laura's music played the old torch songs she knew he enjoyed. Later he packed his few belongings. Con would send his gift of the .357 and its gun-belt to him in Phoenix. He called the airport and made a reservation for a flight home. Shortly after he hung up there was a soft knock at the entrance. He opened the door and gazed at his guest.

"Come in, Roni," he said, I have your laptop right here."

She entered the room wearing a figure-hugging, black, dress with hemline above the knee and belted at the waist. He returned with the computer from the bedroom and stopped. Standing straight, Barkow studied Veronica, staring at her with eyes the color of winter fog rolling over glacial ice. Looking at him, she ignored the icy stare.

The supple fabric clung to the contours of her body as she walked toward him, she angled her head, black eyelashes at half-mast and said, "You know, Michael Taber thinks I'm sexy." Her voice was a throaty purr that easily transmitted competent sex. He recognized the indicators at once.

"Mr. Taber would be a fool not to," he said. "Have you got him stashed on ice somewhere?"

Her smile, somehow reminded Barkow of treachery.

"All it takes is to snap my fingers and he'll come like a trained dog."

"Some are like that," he said. "Others are not."

She ran the tip of her tongue slowly across her upper lip, then purred, "I bet I could make you come."

"Not like a trained dog."

"You could be trained," she stated.

"No, not a chance," his voice dropped from baritone, closer to bass. "What you need is a man who knows how to handle you."

"Would you like to '*handle*' me?"

"If not otherwise involved, perhaps."

The low notes of the CD's tinkling piano lent a romantic mood.

"Damn it Barkow. What do I have to do—beg?"

"No, Roni, just accept defeat. I'm not interested."

"The least you can do is offer a girl a drink."

Barkow set the laptop on a nightstand, then got a glass from the bathroom. He poured in two inches of Blanton's, filled it with ice and handed it to her. "You have the story covered with your paper?"

"Yeah, sure," she said, dis-heartedly. "Got it all nailed down. I'm doing a series on the whole thing. I'll be staying in Belize for at least six weeks."

"Hey kid, don't act so down in the mouth. I like you Roni but I have other commitments."

"Aw you big lug. Why do I always strike out when I find a good one?"

"You've just not found the right one yet, and don't give me that hang dog look." He held her in a brotherly hug. "You'll find your guy when you least expect it.

"I hope so."

He broke the hug and took a card from his wallet. "Here. Give me a call sometime when you need a friend, not a lover."

"What's this, Barkow's Blue Note, thing?"

"I own a small nightclub."

"Okay." She held up her glass in a toast. "Here's to the man that got away." She smiled through tear-filled eyes. They clinked glasses and Barkow said, "And to the prettiest girl in Belize."

They drank. She picked up her laptop and went to the exit. Turning she said, "Bye Barkow, love'ya always."

"You too Roni, see'ya."

She pulled the door closed with a click. Barkow showered and crawled into bed. He lay awake thinking of the day's happenings.

Veronica's a beautiful woman. One I normally would not pass up, but it seems unfair. I'd be crushed if Laura hooked up with some other guy. Maybe some men can cheat, but I'm not one of them. This job's all finished and I'm going home to Laura with a clear conscious.

He awoke to the phone ringing at 3:25 a.m. *Who in the hell is this?* He thought, still half asleep as he reached for the jangling telephone.

"Barkow," he mumbled.

"This is Scotty. I'm giving you a heads-up, man."

"Scotty? Scotty who?"

"Scotty with a capitol C carved into his cheek. That's who."

"Scotty? Leader of the Coyotes? That you?"

"Yeah. That's the one. Your woman wouldn't give me your number, but she told me the hotel you're at. Said if I wanted to call you I should call there."

"Okay, Scotty." Barkow was wide awake now. "What the hell do you want?"

"I got a call from a place called The Bahama's Beauty in Ocho Rio, Jamaica. A Fredrico Morales says he is running Benito's operation since he's been captured in Belize."

"Okay, Scotty. What's that to me?" Barkow growled.

"Same thing as before, man. He wants me to grab your woman."

"And?" Barkow's voice lowered dangerously.

"I guess he's really pissed at you, but it's a different guy then before. You treated me fair and square, even let me keep my cash, last time this was tried, I promised I'd give you a heads up if I heard anything going down that concerns you or yours. That's why I'm calling."

"What's the plan?" Barkow growled into the phone.

"Don't know any more than that. He offered twenty large, but I told him I wasn't interested.

"Good boy, Scotty. You saved yourself a lot of grief. Let me know if you hear any more." Barkow said softly, in an oiled voice. "I'll make it worth your while. Contact Bobby at the Blue Note in Phoenix if you get any more. Don't be callin' my woman, again."

"Alright, will do."

Barkow hung up the phone and called Lieutenant James Greenwell.

"Greenwell," he answered.

"Barkow here, Jim. Sorry I had to wake you. I wanted to let you know that some bozo named Fredrico Morales wants to take over Benito's operation in Ocho Rio, Jamaica, He's trying to hire someone to grab Laura, just like last time. Keep an eye on her for me will you?"

"Sure, I will. Do you know why?"

"Not really, but I'm going over there and find out what Freddie boy has on his mind."

"Okay, Barkow. I'll look in on Laura. When you coming home?"

"Soon as I check this jerk out. You ever hear of him?"

"Nope, I'll ask around and if I dig up anything I'll let you know."

"Thanks, Jim. If you get anything just give the info to Bobby, my bartender at the Blue Note. He'll know how to reach me. Pass the word to Blanco and tell him to keep his eyes peeled, because the Street Dogs calibrated with that gang in Tucson before."

"You mean the Red Coyotes?

"Yeah, in Tucson, but Scotty, the boss down there, owes me now and tipped me off after he refused the offer."

"Okay, see ya later. Take care of yourself."

"Will do. Good night Jim."

Barkow hung up and called Larry Fitzsimmons and Bobby. He filled them in on what was happening and then called Laura.

"Hello, Barkow." She said in a sleep-filled voice. "You coming home early?"

"No Hon. I have some business in Jamaica then I'll be home. Maybe two days.

"Aw, Barkow. Can't you come home, first?"

"No. This has to be nipped in the bud. Some clown is thinking of taking over since we captured his boss. He's so dumb he used the same gang that kidnapped you before. Apparently he wants that same gang to grab you again so he can keep me in check. He's in for a big surprise when I show up. I'll set him straight then come home."

"Dammit, Barkow. Now I'll worry until you call me again."

"Don't be concerned. I'm a big boy and can take care of it. I'll give you a call when I'm on my way."

"Okay, Honey. Should I tell anyone here what is happening?"

"No. I've taken care of that already. I want Larry to keep driving you back and forth to work and Jim will also keep an eye on things.

She sighed. "Damn it anyway. Love you and I'll be waiting."

"Love you too. See you in a few." He hung up the phone.

CHAPTER TWENTY-THREE

BARKOW WAS UP early and checked out of his room. He had breakfast in the hotel restaurant than drove to the airport, turned in his rental and changed his ticket from Phoenix to Ocho Rios. He had two hours to kill so he called Sgt. Conchaco.

"Hi Con."

"Hello, my friend. Are you at home yet?"

"No. I'm still at the Belize Airport. I just wanted to fill you in on some things that happened. I told the company coming to pick up the plane at the temple to call you for advice when they arrived. Right now I have some unfinished business in Jamaica."

"Oh. Something bad happen to Boss man? Can I help?"

"Not really. I just wanted to talk to a friend, unless you're busy?"

"I am never too busy to talk to you. Call me any time."

"Thanks, Con. Remember me telling you about the gang that kidnapped my friend, Laura?"

"Yes. You taught them a lesson in dealing with you."

Barkow chuckled. "Yeah, I did. In fact, it was Scotty, the Tucson gang boss, who called and tipped me off that the same outfit tried to hire him to do the same thing again."

"No kidding?" Con said. "Are they too stupid to remember what happened the time before?"

"Well, Con. It seems they think we captured Benito, the leader of these jerks in Jamaica, with the haul from the Aztec's temple. Now one of the gang underlings is making a move to take over his spot. He must have found some of Benito's papers that outlined the attempted kidnapping of Laura to keep me from coming to Belize."

"He must be crazy in the head to even try again." Con muttered. "By the way, Boss, the Major called me and said that they never found anyone on that river search. They found a place in the jungle where the canoe was pulled up on the bank. They searched the area and found tracks in the mud. Guess what?"

"The Aztec was long gone?"

"Yeah Boss, but they found his tracks in the mud and also the tracks of dress shoes. You know what that means. That Benito gangster had somehow connected with the Aztec. He was the only other one that got away from our trap"

"I wonder if they'll catch them in the jungle."

"So far they can't follow their trail. The Aztec knows how to survive in the jungle and he obviously is making sure Benito don't leave any marks behind."

"Keep me informed on what happens in that situation."

"Will do Boss. What you going to do about the gang in Jamaica?"

"I think that what's left of the gang_don't know the whole story on what went down. I'm flying out of here today for Ocho Rios to nip this thing in the bud. Is there any advice you have on them that I could use? They were a part of the Cortes Syndicate."

"That gang worked out of a bar in Ocho Rios called the *Bahamas Beauty.* Heavy into drugs, prostitution and the local strong-arm stuff. Maybe I can dig up more and call you on the sat phone if I come up with something. When you flying out?"

"About an hour. It's a short flight, only about 750 miles."

"Okay, Boss man. I'll be in touch if I find anything."

"Sounds like a plan Con."

"Bye, Boss. Good luck."

"Bye, Con. Take care." Barkow hung up the phone.

He sat in the loading area for departure to Jamaica and thought about his future plans. Laura was the first thing in his mind.

Sure do miss Laura. I want to get back to her as soon as possible. It would be foolish not to take care of Jamaica right now. Maybe when I get home we can go someplace together. I have no idea where she'd want to go but I'll let her decide. Hopefully she'll not want to go to a Caribbean Island. I've had enough jungle and palm trees for a while…Wonder who the guy in the straw hat is? He seems to be looking at me from time to time.

"Attention: Flight 264 for Jamaica now loading at gate 8," blared the loudspeaker, bringing Barkow out of thoughts of the straw hat. Within fifteen minutes he was among the first passengers aboard the plane and strapped into his first-class seat, prepared for takeoff.

As he waited, slouched in the cushions, he watched from beneath lowered eyelids as the other passengers boarded. Most were obvious tourists, but one man left an impression. He was dressed in casual attire with white trousers, Hawaiian, short sleeved shirt and straw hat. His pale face had the blue-black cast of a clean shaven Italian's heavy beard. With hat pulled down low, his glance darted here and there, back and forth, missing nothing. Barkow did not miss the fact of that gaze hesitating slightly, as it flashed on him a moment, then he moved along to the coach section.

The arrival at the Ian Fleming International Airport in Ocho Rios, happened without incident and Barkow was first off the plane, followed by the other first-class passengers. He quickly walked through the waiting area and turned left to the first boarding gate area for another flight, instead of going right to baggage claim. He watched the Italian come out with a group of coach passengers and began quickly walking and looking here and there as he moved toward baggage claim and exits.

Barkow fell in behind him and saw him enter a men's restroom, only to quickly come back out and hurry down the aisle. He checked a gift shop and continued to the car rental exit, fairly running. Barkow approached him in the car rental garage, talking on a cell phone as he looked up and down rows of rental cars. It was an easy matter to step up behind the fellow and put his left arm around the throat while grabbing the phone hand. He pulled the arm down, then up behind the man's back as the phone went skittering away.

The Italian tried to kick behind him at Barkow's legs. A quick push upward on his arm brought a howl of pain as Barkow's grating voice spoke directly into his ear. "Try that again, stupid, and I'll break your arm. Who were you talking to on the phone?"

"I was calling Frankie, but the call didn't go through."

Barkow walked the man between two cars and shoved him face first against the wall. "Why you tailing me?" He demanded.

"I ain't tailing you, man." Another vicious upward wrench of his arm brought forth a gasp of agony as his face was pushed against the concrete wall. A stream of blood from his nose ran slowly down the wall, collecting on his tropical flowered shirt.

"Okay, okay man." His speech was garbled with his mouth against the wall. "I'm done. You got me."

Barkow pulled him back and spun him around then shoved him back against the wall, knocking the breath from him. He waited a moment for the guy to be able to breathe, then said, "Spill it, asshole, or I'll kill you right here, right now."

"I got a call from Frankie. He wanted me to follow you and see where you go and let him know when you got there. That's all I know. He offered me a single large and airfare."

"How long you worked for Frankie?"

"I don't. He just knew I was in Belize and could do the tail, is all."

"He runs the *Bahamas Beauty*?" Barkow growled.

"Yeah. Word is, he does now."

"Are you carrying?"

"No, man. I got nothin'."

"I'm going to give you some free advice. Do not call Frankie or anyone else about me. Do not go to the Bahamas Beauty and above all, do not ever let me see your ugly face again. If I see you, I'll kill you just like I would a sewer rat. You got that?"

"Yes, sir. I got it and you won't see me ever again."

"Get outa my sight…now."

The Italian stumbled away, thanking his lucky star that he

was still alive. He had never seen the look on a man's face like the one which he had just experienced.

Barkow rented a car and after securing a map of the city, drove out of the airport heading for Ocho Rios. He found Bahamas Beauty Nightclub squatting in a neglected grove of palm trees in the humid Jamaican heat.

He drove through the sun-softened asphalt parking lot surrounding the stucco building and parked beside the only other car on the lot, close to the buildings entrance. Leaving the automobile he approached the front entrance to see a sign hung inside the glass at chest level;

CLOSED: Hours: 7:00 p.m. — 2:a.m.

Barkow grasped the locked door-handle and shook it violently. The sign flopped around inside, but no-one appeared. He walked around the side and in back he found another door. He knocked on the metal sheathed door, his knuckles making little sound. A trash bin and two oil drums stood near the building's back wall. He checked and all were empty except for a few crushed, cardboard boxes in the bin.

"Dammit," he muttered, then noticed a rock, the size of a baseball, where it lay near the drums. Armed with the stone he returned to the door and pounded it against the metal panel, making a satisfying racket.

He heard the click of the lock and the door swung inwards. "Who in the hell are you and what the fuck do ya want?" Demanded a short, heavy-set man in a rumpled white shirt with rolled up sleeves.

Barkow reached in and grabbed a fistful of shirt and stiff-armed the guy into back peddling down a short hallway into the building, slamming him hard against the end wall.

"I wanta talk to whoever's in charge of this dump," He said in a low growl. "Is that you?"

Along one side of the hall an opened case, half full of long-neck, bottled beer, sat on two sealed cases of the same. The worker, with shirt still in Barkow's grip, grabbed a beer bottle by the neck intending to slam it against his antagonist's head until Barkow's fist crashed into his jaw. Both the man and his bottle fell to the floor.

As the bottle rolled away he looked up, glassy eyed, into a face that showed no signs of mercy. He started to get up.

"Stay down," Barkow commanded.

His mistake was to continue to rise. In a swift, hard kick, Barkow's boot thudded against the ribcage of the thug in the white shirt, followed by a grunt of pain. Lesson learned.

"Now then, who's in charge of this place?"

"It used to be Benito," he gasped, "now its Frankie."

"When does Frankie come in?"

"Around six."

"I'll be back at six-thirty." Barkow said. At the door he turned around and looked at the man sitting on the floor holding his aching side. "You tell Frankie boy, I'm coming." He turned and walked out pulling the door shut behind him. He quickly walked around to his car and drove out of the parking lot.

That oughta get the mob together, he thought to himself. He was certain the guy in the white shirt never saw his car so he could not identify it. He drove to a Radio Shack and a Walmart where he picked up a few items including two five gallon gas cans, then stopped by a service station and filled them up. Barkow drove back to the *Bahamas Beauty* and cruised slowly past.

Just like I thought, the car that I'd parked next to, is gone. He drove on around the block and into the blacktop lot, parking behind the building.

It took him nine minutes to pick the two dead-bolt locks and get inside. He quickly cased the main lounge and all the rooms. A small dressing room behind the bandstand, both restrooms and a storage area behind the bar next to the Managers office. From that office, Barkow took a key labeled storage room, that he'd found in a desk drawer. The storage room had several cases of hard liquor and a hot water tank heated with natural gas in the corner. It provided a perfect place to put both cans of gas. He quickly rigged up his homemade bomb using the odds and ends he'd picked up for that purpose. It had a cheap timing device that ignited a wick leading into the taped together cans of gasoline. He set the timer for six-thirty. *This oughta blow half of this building to pieces*, he thought with a single-minded set to his face. He spent a few minutes disguising the explosive device, delighted that the water heater appeared to never been touched for years, having boxes and newspapers piled around it. He gathered any packaging or parts he may have discarded, closed and locked the exit door and drove to a huge beach-front hotel/casino where he secured a room for the night. Relaxing in the room he brought out his new pocket knife and whetstone, then began to slowly put a razor edge on the blade while he watched the afternoon news on TV.

At 5:30 p.m. Barkow was sitting in his car a half-block away watching through recently purchased binoculars, the back door of *Bahamas Beauty*. The gang began to arrive. First came a black SUV that pulled in and parked near the back door. Three men excited; the bartender in white shirt and two tough looking bouncers in rumpled suits. All three went inside. A black Lincoln Towncar roared in at 5:40 and screeched to a stop near the front door.

Barkow watched the driver get out and open the back door. He was a huge black man wearing a Chauffeur's uniform. He held the door open until a tall, thin man wearing a blue suit, with a white vest, shined shoes and a narrow brimmed hat, exited the car. He looked like a gigolo dandy and commanded Barkow's interest. Both men started toward the front door, but now the seven-foot, black giant who followed the gigolo was causing Barkow's memory to catalogue and compare the way he limped, how he held his head at an angle and the roll of his shoulders. From the shadowed haze of recollection this man's features began to crystalize as Barkow brought forth the memory of a savage, giant Haitian, who enjoyed killing, particularly killing women.

The next major surprise arrived in a long, black Cadillac that

thundered into the parking lot with shrieking tires as it negoti-
ated a 360 leaving a cloud of blue rubber smoke in the central
lot and then skidded to a screaming stop. The driver exited the
Caddy and slammed the door shut with a loud *'thunk'*. He wore
a three-piece, dark blue pin-stripe suit, felt dress hat and black
wingtip shoes.

From the other side a large Indian stepped out the car. He
had a long sleeved hoodie that covered most of his face and wore
a pair of cotton trousers and flip-flops.

"Well I'll be damned." Barkow swore as he watched Benito
and the Aztec meet at the back of the car. Benito opened the
trunk lid, letting it spring up in a yawning position. Inside was
a woman with black hair. She was bound hand and foot with
plastic tie-ties. Her mouth was duct-taped shut.

Benito reached in and ruffled the captive's hair. "How was
your ride, Sweetie?" He said as the Aztec watched, stone-faced.
Benito let his hand slide down to fondle her breasts while she
growled in anger behind her taped mouth. "You're going to be a
wild tiger when I get you in bed, you little bitch." He said.

"Leave the trunk open and follow me while I take you in to
meet the boys," he said to the Aztec. "They're going to have quite
a shock when they get a load of me and you."

"Looks like we're going to have a family reunion." Barkow
mumbled to himself.

CHAPTER TWENTY-FOUR

Inside the building, Frankie took the bartender into his office to question him.

"So this guy comes in and roughs you up. What did he look like?

"Like he was one pissed-off dude."

"So, what did he say?"

"Like I told you on the phone, Frankie. He said he was coming back at 6:30 to talk to you."

"Okay. You did like I said and told the gang to be ready to handle this jerk, if he shows up?"

"Yeah, Frankie. They're all here and got their heat with 'em and if Kojo gets hold of this wiseguy, he'll be mincemeat real quick."

"You have the boys beat hell out of him and then bring him in to me. We'll see how tough he really is. I want this handled before seven. You may have to open a little late if it strings out longer. I'm gonna take a quick leak. Tell Kojo to wait in my office for me.

"Okay." The bartender said as he walked to the door. "I'll tell him and then get ready to open at seven."

Unexpectedly, a huge commotion at once began when Benito, followed by the big Aztec, came striding into the club.

"Howdy, boys, hold it right there." Commanded Benito, artillery in hand, as the two bouncers rushed toward them pulling their weapons. The Aztec, knife in hand, dropped into a fighting stance.

"For Christ's sake, Benito," exclaimed the bartender. "We were told you'd been killed or captured by the cops in Belize." Then he shouted, "FRANKIE, get out here—NOW!

Frankie rushed out of the office and went to the group of men who stood staring at each other. "HOLD ON," Frankie bellowed. "GODAMNIT, we're on the same side here. Put the guns away and let's talk."

Benito stared at Frankie. "Who the fuck put you in charge, eh Frankie? I run things in this gang and I'll decide what we do and how we do it."

"Well, shit, Benito. I thought you were dead or captured so I been running things for you until you came back. It's your show, so do it your way. No problem, I'm good with that."

"You damn well better be," Benito growled. "This is a new member," he nodded toward the Aztec.

One of the bouncers stepped forward and put out his hand to the Aztec, who snarled and feinted with the knife, causing the bouncer to leap back.

"You can call him Aztec. He's a mite touchy so I suggest you leave him alone."

While the gang members were beginning to understand that Frankie was out and Benito was in and they were going to have the Aztec for a gang member, Kojo came from the office, into the room. He sized up the Aztec whose only response was to put a sneer on his face as he spat on the floor. A sign of disrespect.

Frankie said, "I gotta take a leak", as he walked across the dancefloor to the restroom.

"Kojo," Benito said, "come into my office. You also, Aztec. I want you two to get to know each other because I got a little surprise out in my car who's going to provide us with a very special party." The two huge men followed the leader of the *Bahamas Beauty* gang into the office.

The time was six-thirty. Kojo and Aztec listened to Benito as he began talking in the office. The other men sat on barstools watching the barkeep prepare his bar for the night's business. In the dusty corner of the water-heater storage room, next to the office, the timer tripped a switch which ignited the black powder in the center of the waxed wick that led over the threaded lip and into the first gasoline can. The fire crept slowly, melting the wax and burning the wick, creeping closer and closer up and finally into the fumes drifting out of the open spout of the can—the room exploded.

The entire storage room, the bar area and the office blew into smithereens, taking half the roof with it. The wreckage at once broke out in flames as Frankie staggered from the restroom. He was the only person left alive because he had been isolated from the blast across the dance floor by the restroom walls. He ran the length of the remaining dancefloor, through the front entrance heading straight for the Lincoln. He tried to open the driver's door but the car was locked. He hastily searched his pockets until he remembered that Kojo had the car keys. He stared at the remains of the *Bahamas Beauty*. Half the building was completely destroyed by the blast with tongues of flame licking at the remainder. A man appeared in the fire lighted, evening air. Frankie stood in shocked awe as the new arrival stepped before him and with a single blow, knocked him down.

Barkow, reached down and grabbed Frankie by his white vest and hauled him up, pushed his back against the Lincoln and leaned in close. As they stood there face to face, Barkow said in a gruff, menacing voice, "Frankie boy. If I ever see your ugly face again, I'll kill you. You're nothing but a two-bit piece of shit. I want your oath that you or yours will never bother me or mine again. You got that?"

"Yeah, I got it. You have my oath, uh, Sir," mumbled a shocked Frankie.

Barkow drew forth his pocket knife and opened the blade.

"My name's Barkow, Laura's my girl. So, say it like you mean it or I'll carve you up right now."

All the bravado deserted Frankie as he stuttered, "I g-got it Mr. Barkow. I p-promise you'll never see me again and you have my o-oath to never bother or a-attack you or yours again," his voice shaky, as fear for his life made him tremble.

Barkow reached out with the knife and touched Frankie's

quivering cheek with the tip of the blade. He cut a three quarter circle the size of a silver dollar in the cheek. "That C is to remind you, just how committed to that oath, you will be."

"I-I-I'm committed," he stammered. "I promise. You'll n-never see me again."

Barkow left him standing in stunned shock beside the locked Lincoln with blood flowing down his cheek to drip from his jawline. He quickly walked back to his car and drove out, headed towards his hotel. A twisted smile contorted his face, as two police squad cars rushed past him in the opposite direction, sirens blearing, lights flashing.

Back in his room at the hotel/casino, Barkow let his hatred fade away until his breathing was under control and *The Chains of love* melody, those background strains of sad, heart-broken music that always swirled in the background of his mind when rage and anger took control. Eventually, he called the airport and purchased a ticket for Phoenix; then called Laura at the Blue Note.

"Hello," came the answer. "This is Laura. May I help you?"

"Hi Laura," he said. "I'm leaving on a 7:15 a.m. flight for Phoenix tomorrow morning. I should be in around noon and be at the condo by twelve-thirty."

"Oh, Barkow. That's wonderful," she said in an excited voice. "How I've missed you. I'll be waiting at the condo for you."

"Missed you too," he said. "Is everything alright?"

"Everything is fine now that you're coming home. It's time for my first set of the evening, so I need to run."

"Okay. Hon. I'll see you tomorrow."

"Goodbye, darling. I love you."

"Until tomorrow, then."

☉ THE POLICE CAME and called in a fire report and an ambulance for the bleeding man. Later a wrecker towed the black SUV away to a police holding lot. Due to a paperwork foul up, they never came back for the Lincoln or the Cadillac. The black

Cad was pilfered a few nights later. The Lincoln was stripped of all saleable parts by a gang of juvenile youths.

Nine days after Barkow flew away from Jamaica, a white, late model, rented Cadillac turned into the Ocho Rios property that had housed the *Bahamas Beauty* nightclub. The lone occupant pulled up to the charred wreckage of the club. The Caddy's front door opened and a man stepped out. He looked at the remains of the building. The windows in the still-standing, unburned portion, were blown out. The entrance stood open with its door, hinged side down and hanging from the dead-bolt locks still attached to a twisted, steel doorframe.

The right-hand enforcer, of the richest woman in the world, stood looking at the demolished building. He was a study in angles, from his sharply blocked, felt, dress hat above the harsh plane of his overhung brow, to the squared shoulders of the immaculately tailored black suit. The trousers held a knife-blade crease that broke perfectly on highly shined dress shoes with squared off toes. Starched white cuffs extended exactly one inch beyond the end of his jacket sleeves. He looked and acted like a highly positioned executive, in total control.

Jacques walked over to the stripped-out Lincoln with the windows cracked or shattered. The tires and wheels, including the spare, were missing. The dash was full of empty holes where the electronics had been removed. Even the headlamps had been taken. He peered inside at the tattered upholstery and empty space where the rear seat cushion used to be. Jacques turned away, walked to the Cad and peeled out of the lot, heading to a real estate office.

The broker of the company was hired to have someone demolish and haul away the remnants' of the building, its foundation, the asphalt pavement and everything else on the lot, including the junked Lincoln. He was also to have a grader come in and grade the land so it was presentable.

The realtor was told to erect a decent sized *For Sale* sign on the property and sell it for whatever it was worth. They agreed on his fee of 6% and the price of having the construction work done. The broker was paid in cash and given a copy of the title to the property, including an Axelwood Properties business card of who to contact for the genuine title when he obtained a buyer.

With smoking tires creating an acrid smell of burnt rubber, the white Cadillac peeled away from the curb on its way to the airport.

CHAPTER TWENTY-FIVE

As THE JUMBO Jet made preparations for getting underway from Jamaica to Arizona, Barkow sat relaxing in the comfortable seat cushions of his first class accommodations. He called Con and filled him in on what had happened during his stay in Jamaica. He told of his surprise, seeing Benito and the Aztec go into the club building.

"Benito and the Aztec were there, in Jamaica?"

"Yes. I was shocked to see them show up."

"What did you do?"

"They went into the club and I hurried over to the Cadillac with the raised trunk lid and of all people there was Lola."

"Who? Lola who?" Con, now excited, asked.

"Lolita Vito, the daughter of Vito the helicopter pilot. Remember he had sent them to Jamaica for safety."

"Yes, I remember. How did that happen?"

"I quickly hustled her over to my car. Somehow Benito had found out Lola and her mother had been sent by Vito to Jamaica to be safe. I removed the duct tape she was bound with. Apparently the Aztec got Benito safely out of the jungle and then Benito got the Aztec safely to his gang in Jamaica. With his connections here, he found where Lola and her mother were staying and grabbed her. Funny how things work out sometimes."

"Man, Barkow. Nothing funny about that Indian. It's a good thing you saved Lola."

"Yes. She and her mother are flying for Belize today. I gave them some money for tickets."

"That's great. I'll call Vito, but I'm sure he has already heard from her. What happened with the gang in the club?"

"I took care of the problem. Only Frankie got out alive. I sent him on his way after a friendly conversation."

"I see," Con said. "I know how friendly you can be, my friend. Thank God you were able to help."

"This plane is ready to take off, Con. I got to hang up. I'll call you later, Brother, when I get home."

"Ok, Brother. Fly safe, I'll talk with you soon." Con cut the connection.

Barkow's flight from Jamaica approached Sky Harbor Airport in a long, gliding run. The pilot set the wheels down on the runway with barely a tremor. He deplaned as soon as possible and headed straight for the long-term parking lot. As time marked 12:35 p.m. he was pulling into his condo's basement parking space. He left the Mercedes, punched the lock button on his key-remote and heard the answering horn-blast as the alarm and locking system engaged. He stepped into the elevator and rode to the lobby of the huge building.

Barkow smiled when he saw Henry Harrison reading his ever present paperback. "Hi Hank," he said as he stepped up to the counter.

"Hey, Barkow. Hi and welcome home. Looks like you're all in one piece. Did you have a good trip?"

"Yeah, thanks, everything went according to plan. Are things alright around here?"

"Quiet as a mortuary. I haven't heard a peep out of anyone for days. Miss Laura comes and goes every day but Sunday. She's got that actor, Larry, following her around like a lovesick puppy. He drives her to and from work every day."

"Good. I set that up before I left. I'm glad all is quiet. It's great to be back. I'll see you later Hank." Barkow said as he headed for the elevator. It was 12:55 p.m. when he unlocked the door to his penthouse and stepped inside. Laura was sitting in a huge leather recliner when she heard the door open. She tossed the book on the floor and dashed to meet Barkow coming through the entrance into the room.

She was wearing a blue and white skirt that swirled around her legs as she rushed to Barkow and pressed herself against him while being gathered into his arms. They stood locked in a tight embrace. Barkow could smell the gardenia scent of her body-spray as he buried his face in her honey-gold hair. He felt her breasts pushing against his chest and suddenly she broke into soft crying as she plastered him with kisses. With tears streaming down her face she began to talk between kisses. "I'm...so glad you're home...I've missed you so much...I'm so happy...I finally have you in my arms."

He bent slightly and scooped her off her feet and began walking through the huge living room, She was kissing and crying and muttering "I love you," again and again, until he sat down on a couch with her on his lap. He found her mouth with his and through parted lips, he slipped his tongue. So began the dueling contest as hers met his with equal eagerness. Her mouth slid to his throat as she nibbled and kissed his neck. Laura ended up with her head on his lap until he again pulled her up and found her mouth with his.

"God. Laura, your kisses are so damn good," he mumbled.

"Yours too, darling. I feel like we could do this forever. I love you so much my whole body trembles just thinking of you. Are you tired after such a long trip away from me? Let me fix you a drink, are you hungry?"

"I'm hungry for you," he groaned. "I just want to hold you and feel you and look at you."

"What you need is a drink before you get carried away."

It would be impossible for me not to be attracted to her sexually, he thought, but said "Perhaps a drink would be good."

"Yes, perhaps." She said as her eyelids lowered to half-mast. She slipped from his lap and stood before him, breathing rapidly with a flushed face. "I'd better fix us both a drink before I start luring you into the bedroom." She went into the den and presently came back with two highball glasses filled with bourbon and ice cubes. She leaned over to hand Barkow his glass, offering an excellent view of her breasts, now loosely slung in a bra. His eyes regretfully disengaged from staring at the partially hidden delights seducing him and looked into her eyes, glowing with evidence he could have anything he wanted.

She sat beside him and said seriously, "Tell me all about your trip and all the pretty girls you came across."

"None as beautiful as you," he spoke softly. "I could be happy, simply adoring you, but unsatisfied."

"Adoration is sweet but you're right. It's unsatisfying. I want to satisfy all of you," she said in a husky whisper. "All of you, your body and soul and everything else. I want to give you all a woman can give a man. I want to be enslaved by you, Barkow. I've loved you for years."

"All the time I've been away," he said. "You were on my mind. I tried to forget you so I could do my job, but I couldn't. My first love ended in such confusion, and distrust, and hatred, I thought I could never love again. I tried, Laura, so hard not to fall for you, because I was terrified, thinking it could never be. I was afraid I would somehow ruin it, and you could never love me in the same way I would love you. If that happened I would die a thousand deaths, before I took my life. We must go slowly, Laura. I think I love you, but my thoughts are so chaotic and confused about committing to real, honest love again. Give me some time to heal myself after that woman tore my entire world apart. Can you do that? Can you honestly wait until I know in my heart, that I can love you wholly and completely without a shred of doubt?"

"I'll wait as long as it takes." Laura said. "Loving you is my life and I so want you to love me the same way, if it takes a year or a decade I'll be waiting for you to tell me you do. Until then, she smiled, we can get to know each other in every way a man and woman can. There will be no legal commitment by either of us until you initiate it.

"Thank you, Miss Laura. Thank you for being kind, sweet and understanding." With that said, Barkow began to tell her about his recent trip to Belize. He told her everything he had done. He told it all. She let him say, what she knew he had to say. She listened patiently and asked no questions; knowing he needed to tell it all in his own way.

"Remember, I told you before, Laura. I'd loved a woman named Mary, who'd been kidnapped and taken to the Island of St. Lucia in the Caribbean. They'd locked her in a private retreat deep in the jungle. The man in charge of that retreat was named Kojo, a seven foot, depraved drunk, addicted to rum and torturing women. He was of pure Haitian decent, and deeply involved in voodoo crime but escaped from Haiti, to the island of St. Lucia. I'd gone to rescue Mary and in doing so, I'd beaten Kojo to the point of death and actually thought the giant had crawled off into the jungle and died. I used the same type of homemade bomb to blow up that retreat as I'd rigged in the *Bahamas Beauty*."

"Something else you need to know, Laura. I've been trained by the CIA in a sub-secret, service called Delta Force in the United States Army. I know twenty-one ways to kill a man with my bare hands. I'm exceptionally proficient at self-preservation and highly efficient in all tactics of offense and defense. Recently I came across Kojo, in Jamaica. It brought back a memory of love for Mary, until she did the most despicable and unthinkable thing a woman could do to a man."

"It doesn't matter." She whispered. "Let the past remain where it is and we will go on from here. I'll pack up my things and move back to my apartment."

"I've also been thinking about that," he said. "Why not move in here with me on a permanent basis? There's plenty of room."

"But Barkow, I have a Grand piano, my antique, roll-top wine and music cabinet and absolutely tons of clothing. My shoes alone would fill your closet."

"Nonsense, I have it all figured out. You know, Laura, I own the entire penthouse floor of this building. Half of it is empty. We can make it into your private suite of rooms. You can move in any of the furniture pieces you want to keep and give the rest to Goodwill. We can pick out any other items you'd like to furnish it with, or simply have an interior decorator come in and do it all. Whatever you want. You can have your own private entrance, but I'd want it interconnected with my rooms."

"Essentially, the same thought occurred to me," Laura said, "but I declined to mention it because I didn't want it to become a difficult situation between us."

"It's settled then. You'll move into the penthouse and I'll furnish whatever else you need."

"Oh, Barkow, how I love you."

"As I do you. Now let's go for dinner. What time do you go to work at the Blue Note?"

"I normally go in around 4:00 and work in the office until 7:00 when my first set begins. I work my show until 11:00. On weekends I stay with the show until midnight."

"How much time do you actually need to stay on top of everything that a manager keeps track of?'

"I could do all of it easily in one hour instead of three. I just go in that early when you're not here."

"Good," he muttered. "I plan to take up a lot of your time. What is the slowest day for business at the club?"

"Monday and Tuesday are about the same for being slow, then business picks up from there, building through Friday and Saturday, then falls off Sunday. Bobby kept the bar open every day."

"Okay, Madam Manager," he beamed. "Give everyone a raise, including yourself and you are to begin taking Monday and Tuesday off. Close the Blue Note down on Sundays. Bobby can handle the place when you're not there and if he needs help, even part time, you can hire someone for that position, when needed."

Laura sat beside him. She smiled and said, "It sounds like you've been giving this a lot of thought."

"I have," he said as he returned her smile. "Who cleans the place?"

"What do you mean?"

"Who vacuums the carpets, sweeps and mops the floors and cleans the bathrooms?"

"Oh. We all do that on Monday after the place closes." She laughed.

"Hire a cleaning service to take care of that on Sunday when the place is closed. Put Bobby in charge of seeing that it's done correctly."

"Okay, Boss." She said with a smile.

"I will no longer be your boss," Barkow said, looking at Laura's shocked stare.

"What does that mean?" she said in a small voice.

"It means, I am making you an equal partner in the Blue Note. We will be co-owners with equal rights concerning the business."

"Aww, Barkow. You don't need to do that. I like being a singing manager."

He reached over and pulled her to him. "It's settled. I'll have the papers drawn up right away."

"What if I refuse to sign?" She teased.

"In that case I would seduce you into signing them. It would be fun."

She would have answered but his mouth was on hers and she forgot about responding. They broke apart for air. He murmured, "I love everything about you, Laura. The perception of you, the fragrance, the guise and the sound of you. He again softly touched his lips to hers.

CHAPTER TWENTY-SIX

T HEY DROVE TO Valentino's. "Remember this place?" Barkow said.

"How could I forget? This is where you took me on our first date."

Barkow and Laura dined in a raised section of the restaurant a foot higher than the dance floor. They ordered Dinner while a three-piece band moaned a bluesy sound.

"May I have this dance," Barkow asked in his low baritone. She smiled, nodded and rose from the table. He led her to the dance floor and hand in hand, they walked across to the musicians. Barkow held up a fifty-dollar bill to the bandleader and requested, "*Chains of Love,* by solo trumpet." They slow-danced in and out of the shadows, the only couple on the darkened floor,

"I'll never forget how romantic this place will forever be to me." Laura said as she danced with her head against Barkow's shoulder.

"And I'll never forget how beautiful you looked that night," Barkow spoke in a low voice. "You wore a pale-jade gown that set your green eyes off to perfection," he said. "You look just as lovely tonight."

They returned to their table, causing the head-waiter to snap his fingers and at once a serving waiter in black tux pushed a small cart soundlessly to their table, from which he served their meal. The food was exquisitely prepared and served.

They finished, sans dessert and Laura said, "I need to be at the club for my first set, which starts at seven, if we are to keep the clientele happy."

"We have time for another dance," Barkow stated. He

took her hand and once more led her onto the shadowed floor. Like magic, *The Chains of Love*, at once began to throb in a low, mournful melody on a lone trumpet. They danced, molded to one another, the only couple on the floor.

Arriving at *Barkow's Blue Note Nightclub* at 6:55 p.m, Laura went straight to the grand piano. The soft patter of polite clapping sounded at once from the seated customers. She smiled and nodded at several of the regulars and began a soft, romantic rendition of *Stardust*.

Barkow sat at the reserved table. It stood slightly isolated from the other tables, had a raised, lettered bronze *RESERVED* device with a built-in, electrically lighted candle situated at its center and two comfortable chairs. Terry threaded through the customer tables and came directly toward Barkow. He stood up as she arrived.

"Hi Barkow, welcome home."

"Hi Terry. It's good to be back," he said as he hugged her. "How are things going with you and Bobby?"

"Just great." She said as she set down his customary drink of Blanton's bourbon, on the rocks.

"Gotta run. I see someone who wants a refill." She swept away to her customer.

Barkow smiled and waved at Bobby the bartender, who gestured back. Beautiful piano music engulfed the room and Laura's clear, sensual voice sang every other song. In fifteen minutes she took a break and sat down with Barkow.

"How long does your set last?" he said.

"It mostly depends on how tired I am. Sometimes I use 20 minutes on and 20 off and other times, if I'm in the mood, I'll sing until closing time."

"Do any of the customers try to hit on you?"

"Not any of the regulars. They know I don't drink when I'm singing and Bobby is not bashful about setting anyone straight when they want to order a drink sent over to me. One night a guy got quite drunk and was hitting on Terry until she told him off and then he started pestering me. When I went to my office, on a break, he followed me there. Terry told Bobby and he came in and whacked the guy on the head with a fifth of whisky, then threw him out the front door. Everybody clapped.

"He got off lucky. I know Bobby knows how to handle himself in a brawl."

"The word is out that I'm your girl and that's enough to scare most of the troublemakers away."

"Good," Barkow said. "Do you think we need a bouncer?"

"No. This is too nice a place for any major problem like that. You'll notice almost every customer wears a suit and the women are dressed to the nines."

Barkow and Laura stayed the entire evening at the club. They talked during her breaks and he spent some time chatting with Bobby while she sang, providing he was not busy with customers. Several of the regulars came by to introduce themselves and remark how very nice the Blue Note was and all commented on Laura's singing. A number of them advised him to never change the 50's style of music. After they closed for the night, all four of the 'Blue Notes' went out for a sandwich and coffee. It was obvious that Terry and Bobby were in love with each other.

"There was a phone call from the same man several times, who simply asked for Mr. Barkow and always wanted to know when you would be back in town," Bobby said. "I told him to keep trying because I thought it would not be long. He always thanked me and hung up. Didn't want to leave any message."

"Who knows?" Barkow said. "Could be anyone."

"Next time he calls, you want me to ask for a number and tell him you'll call?"

"You can try that, Bobby, but I doubt he will. From what you told me of his calls, he don't want to tip off who he is or where he's from."

"Come on, Bobby," Terry said. "I'm beat. Let's go home."

"Yeah, me too. Welcome home, Barkow, see you and Laura later."

Both couples left the diner and drove away in opposite directions.

"It's been a wonderful day having you home again." Laura said as she leaned across the center console and laid her head against Barkow's shoulder. "You'll never know how lonely I've been when you're away."

"No need to be lonely anymore. In fact you'll probably get tired of me hanging around all the time."

"Don't be silly. I love being with you. I've secretly dreamed of us being together forever and always.

The black Mercedes sped through the night and eventually drove into the basement parking area of the penthouse building. They took the elevator to the lobby, waved at Hank and went straight up to the penthouse.

"I'm ready for a shave and hot shower." Barkow said. "How about you?"

"I don't need a shave but a shower would be nice." Laura said in a soft and sultry voice that held a suggestion of underlying passion and sensuality.

"Ladies first," he said with a smile and opened the door to the master bedroom's oversized bathroom.

She giggled and said, "I've been using the guest bedroom and bath."

"That don't work anymore. We'll have to make do with this."

"Is that so? You'd think me a tramp if I agreed to shower in a man's private bathroom, without so much as an argument."

"There's a closet with soaps, shampoos, hairnets, towels and all the needed paraphernalia for taking a bath. What more could you ask for?"

"I could say, privacy, but I'd not wish to scare you off." She said in a husky purr, conveying proficient sensual overtones.

"I don't scare easily," his voice a low baritone as he stared at her and imagined her nude, obtainable and available. In that moment he also knew, like all women, she could be dangerous.

"Scaring you is not what I intend to do." She murmured as

she strode past him through the bathroom doorway, leaving a soft scent of gardenia in her wake.

He pulled the bath door shut and went into the bedroom. He sat on a chair with a built-in valet stand. His body, still stiff with desire, as he bent and removed his shoes and socks. He stood and slowly removed his clothing, hanging his suit on the mahogany valet stand, putting his pocket things in the drawer and then walked back into the large, luxurious bathroom.

The room was filling with steam as he brushed his teeth and rinsed his mouth with mouthwash. After shaving, he entered the shower through the warm, muggy air rolling out of the snail-shell entrance. The shower's walls had ten water jets advantageously located so hot water spewed from every direction. All were opened to a high pressure, creating a cloudy steamed vision of Laura's beautiful body, perfectly suntanned to a peaches and cream complexion.

Barkow put his arms around her, pulling her naked body against him. His mouth found hers, immediately creating arousal. He felt the brush of her nipples on his chest.

"Want to soap me down? Then I'll do you." She said in a low suggestive voice.

"I think I can handle that." He whispered in a revealing voice and turned the water jets to emit a curling fog, including that one directly overhead.

As a cloud of warm fog billowed and swirled around them, he pushed the petal handle of a built-in soap dispenser, filling his hand with an abundant mound of lathered soapsuds. He turned to the blurred form of Laura and wiped the foamy lather across a shoulder and the upper slopes of her breasts then moved behind her. Reaching around, his large hands each cupped a breast and began to gently massage the warm, slippery, scented suds over them. The protruding buds centered in her large, dark areolas drew into firmness as his thumbs slid slowly, back and forth, across the swelling nipples.

She pushed back against him, her body slightly trembling.

Her firm, breasts now weighed perfectly in his palms. His hands slipped downward, collecting lather, and slowly rubbed across a trim waist, then circled her small, firm belly.

Laura, now literally panting as his fingers edged lower to circle her navel and brush across the mat of golden-brown pubic hair. She pushed her rump against that hard, lean body, feeling his aroused condition as his hand slipped farther down; lightly touching the crease of womanhood, slowly tracing it downward.

With a gasp she turned to face him, lifting her arms around him with fingers combing through his thick, black hair. Her body crushed against his as their lips met in a hot, almost brutal, kiss. Jolts of response throbbed low in her center. His kiss grew rough, then nearly cruel. Barkow wanted to drag her to the floor and forcefully ram himself into her, hard and vicious until her screams echoed like cannon salvos and his release erupted like hot, thick blood. It would be quick, violent and over.

"Barkow! You're hurting me." She grunted into his ear. He suddenly released her and pushed her toward the exit.

"Go. I'll be right out." He said, breathing heavily as he turned the jets back to ejecting water.

Laura pecked him on the lips and went into the bathroom. She used a huge, white towel to dry off and was working on her hair when unexpectedly, she realized he was standing in the entrance to the shower watching her.

He was trying to understand how she could be so modest; she looked too perfect, too flawless and too gorgeous. How could such an absolute phenomenon of feminine beauty be interested in him? "There's a hair dryer inset in the wall," was all he could think of to say.

She smiled and walked over to him. "I love you, Barkow, with all my heart and soul." Throwing her arms around his neck she placed a long, loving kiss upon his surprised face.

"I love you too," he said. "I love you so much I couldn't bear the thought of hurting you. Are you alright?"

"Of course I'm alright, Darling. Dry off and get in bed. I'll make my hair presentable and join you in a few."

He smiled and toweled himself off, then went from the bathroom to the bar and picked up a cold bottle of champagne, a bucket of ice, two champagne flutes, also a few candles and returned to the bedroom. He positioned a lighted candle on a night stand between two easy chairs. The bucket of iced champagne was put by the candle. A few more were scattered around the room creating a soft candlelight glow. He turned on soft music and started the gas fireplace. Lastly, he removed the comforter and massive pillows from the California King, then turned the covers down over the foot of the bed, leaving only the blood-red, satin sheet and four equally cased pillows. As he was placing robe and slippers by each side of the bed, Laura came into the bedroom.

"Umm," she said. "This looks like the den of iniquity my mother warned me about."

"Tis a love nest for you, fair maiden," he murmured, "where I shall lead thee gently down the path of love."

"I'm inexperienced in the realm of love, kind Sir, and you must treat me gently with kindness and promise never-ending love, to broach my capable fortifications."

"Consider it promised fair one, thee has but to come," he snickered, "with me, and thou shall have both kindness and never ending love."

"In that case, I shall come." Together they slipped onto the huge bed and she at once curled up with her back against his body. Laura had dried and combed her dark-golden hair into its natural waves and swirls. Her skin was still warm from the shower, damp in crevice of knee, thigh and elbow. He could smell the blending of shampoo with soap and powder, mixed with the scent of her flesh masked by the lingering ghost of gardenias.

He moved aside, rolled her on her back and placed his lips to hers, finding them open and inviting. He spoke in a voice thick with passion. "Laura, I'm the luckiest man in the world, to have a woman, such as you to love me; allowing me to love in return."

"I've always loved you, Babe, from the first time I saw you. You were trying to drink yourself to death in that horrible bar where I worked."

"Like you said, Laura, let's forget the past and begin our lives on a new slate. Let bygones remain in the 'used to be'. I'll love you as no man ever loved a woman in the past, present or future. I'll never cheat, lie, or go behind your back. I'll respect you in all the ways a man can. I can protect you against the world and I will love and cherish you forever. All I ask is you will love me the same way."

"It's always been that way for me, Barkow."

He cupped his hand over a breast and drew it's rosebud into his mouth. He gently pressed the breast forcing the nipple to extend. He could feel it swell and lengthen in his mouth as her hand slipped downward over the abdominal muscles of his flat stomach, finding virility.

They explored one another between kisses and tender words of love. Each quickly discovered their partner to be a replica of their dreamed desire and both consciously and subconsciously, of what they wanted. In the process of their journey of discovery, each became so instilled with passion that no earthly power could stop the advancement. It began by her saying between short, quick breaths, "You want to? You want to do me, Honey?

He mumbled, "Can I? Can I have you, all of you? I need you so much."

"Do it. Do it now...I can't wait...hurry, Honey, do it now, right now."

He hovered above as she spread herself and clasped her hands behind him when he settled into place.

"I'm going to do you, Laura," he gasped

"Yes, yes, I want it...now, Honey, now...."

He pushed into her as slowly as he could hold himself back. It was as if they both were regulated to the same degree of passion. A craving so great that nothing could or would hold back the inevitable outcome.

"Tell me you love me." He gasped into her ear, prolonging the deluge.

"I love you, Darling." She panted. "Honey, I love you. She breathed the words meeting each thrust with an upwards push. "Say it again." He could feel her muscles grip him like an embracing fist, gritting his teeth to keep from exploding, he said, "Tell me again." "I love you…love…love" He felt her muscles grip and tense, felt and heard a shuddering sob of gushing release and then allowed himself to empty heart, soul and seed into her body.

CHAPTER TWENTY-SEVEN

DAYS FLEW PAST in a whirlwind of getting to know each other on a more private basis, planning ideas for Laura's apartment addition and having all her personal property put in storage until she was ready to move in. Construction plans were drawn up, a contractor was hired and a start date was agreed upon. Barkow purchased a new Lexus for Laura and they made many trips to upgrade-furniture stores and boutiques. It became their custom to have dinner together prior to Laura going to the Blue Note on her workdays. The new business hours pleased Bobby and Terry with Sundays off. The four of them occasionally went to operas and ballets. One day the mysterious phone call again came to Bobby, once more asking for Barkow.

"Are you available to meet him tonight, at seven?" Bobby said.

"Where would he want to meet?" Came the answer.

"Here, at the club."

"I'll be there at seven."

"Okay, I'll inform him to expect you. What's your name?"

His answer was a click as the caller hung up. Barkow and Laura came in at six. She worked in her office for a while, as Barkow talked with Bobby.

"This guy does not want anyone to know anything about him, including his name." Bobby said.

"Yeah, and that makes me suspicious right away. If you think you can pick him out when he comes in, give me a heads up. I'll be in my office and can get a look at him through closed circuit." Barkow said. "I'm glad we had that video system put in because it covers both interior and the parking lot."

"It'll be a god-send if we ever get held up or broken into. Talk to you later. Boss." Bobby walked down the bar to a customer. "What'll you have?"

Barkow drifted away to Laura's office and found her in the process of leaving.

"The place is filling up," He said. "How're you doing?"

"I'm done, if you'd like to sit at our table in the lounge."

"We can for a while, but I want to be in my office when my guest arrives."

They went to the reserved table and sat down. Barkow motioned for Terry to come over and ordered Blanton's on the rocks and for Laura, a club soda. She never drank hard liquor when she was working. At 6:45 the lights lowered. Happy hour was over. They made small talk until Laura said, "See you later, Honey." She sauntered over to the grand piano. Barkow went back to his office.

He turned a monitor on, showing six small views of interior and exterior of the Blue Note Nightclub. A limousine was just pulling into the curb at the front door. The driver exited and went around to open the back passenger door. The man who climbed out was of medium build and wearing a dark suit. He said something to the driver and walked to the front door.

Barkow shifted his gaze to the interior view of the nightclub entrance, just as the man came in and headed for the bar. Bobby spoke into the intercom to Barkow's office, "Heads up, Boss." Then went to meet the stranger at the end of the bar.

Looking at the stranger on the monitor, Barkow did not recognize him. He was ordinary looking in all respects. No facial hair, perhaps 40 years old and well dressed. Bobby picked up the house phone.

"Your guest is here. Want me to bring him back?"

"Yes, please." Barkow answered and watched the monitor as the Bartender led the man toward his office. Presently a knock sounded. He opened the door and said, "Come in. Thanks Bobby." The man walked in.

"Hello, my name is Barkow, G. B. Barkow and you are?"

"Hello Mr. Barkow, I'm Victor E. Schmidt." They shook hands and Barkow motioned toward the chair before his desk. "Have a seat Mr. Schmidt. What can I do for you?"

"You can listen to a little proposition the United States Government would like to make to you." He sat in the chair and crossed his legs.

Barkow sat behind his desk.

"What sort of proposition?"

"The government has spent a great deal of time looking into your past history. We know you're a trained specialist in covert operations by the Delta Force, sub- secret branch of the CIA. According to their files you were one of the very best they had. Are you willing to tell me why you chose to be discharged after six years?"

"Why would that information be of interest to you, Schmidt?"

"Why would you not wish to tell me, Barkow?"

"I don't think of it as being any of your business, as yet?"

"I see." He took a card from his inner pocket and handed it to Barkow.

Barkow looked at the card, *Victor E. Schmidt, CIA Director, United States of America.* He flipped it onto his desk top. "So you're the director of CIA. So What?"

"I need to know if you quit because you lost your nerve, that's all"

"My nerve is just fine, Schmidt. Since that's all, you know your way out."

"Oh, but we're not finished Mr. Barkow. You have not heard the proposition yet."

"Listen Schmidt. If you want to waste time, go find someplace else to ask questions. You come in here like you want to make a big impression. If you got something to say, stop beating around the damn bush and spit it out. Otherwise get the hell out of my office."

Schmidt smiled at Barkow. "Okay, Barkow. Here's the deal.

The CIA needs a civilian who can think on his feet. A man who can take matters into his own hands when it's needed. Someone who is not afraid of danger and will kill when necessary. You'd be well compensated in cash and would only be called on when we needed a person of your expertise. One with no ties to the government. Special cases that require a tough sonofabitch who we know we can trust to get the job done and done right. All expenses paid plus monthly wages, bonus's and all benefits included. You would only be called on rare occasions, perhaps once or twice a year. That's the deal with a five million dollar life insurance thrown in.

"Okay. I'll think it over." Barkow said as he stood up.

"Is that all you have to say?"

"Give me your number and I'll call when I make up my mind."

"I'll call you in a few days for your answer. May I have your card?" Schmidt said and remained in his seat. Barkow sat back down.

"Tell you what, Schmidt. Forget the whole thing. You refuse to offer a contact number. You give me a business card and act like some hot-shot used to having people run scared whenever you utter a word or two. I don't jump through hoops for anyone, unless I know a hell of a lot more then you're willing to give. I'm at present, under the impression, you're trying to pull some sort of con game. Go tell whoever you take orders from, it's no dice. There's the door you came in and you can leave the same way. Now get out before I throw you out."

"Now listen, Barkow I will not...."

Barkow stood up unexpectedly, slamming his chair against the wall and pointed at the door. "OUT!" He barked.

Barkow's phone rang. He picked up the receiver and heard Bobby's voice.

"Looks like he left in a huff, Boss. Is everything alright?"

"Yeah, its okay, Bobby. I doubt we'll ever hear from him again."

"That's good. See you later, Boss."

Barkow sat at his desk and considered what Schmidt had

told him. He decided if there was anything of truth to it, he would hear from someone about it. He called Lieutenant James Greenwell, a detective in the Phoenix Police Department.

"Greenwell."

"Hi Jim, Barkow here. You busy?"

"Hey, Barkow. What Can I do for you?"

"You ever heard of a guy named Victor E. Schmidt?"

"Not off the top of my head. What's up?"

"He's been calling the club for me and would not leave a name or contact number. Tonight he showed up and gave me a business card that said he was a Director of CIA in the US Government and wanted to hire me."

"That's easy enough to trace. You want me to run a sheet on him?"

"I thought he was a phony. I'd appreciate it if you would."

"Not a problem."

"We need to get together and have dinner or something, Jim."

"Yeah, that sounds like a good idea."

"I'm talking just friends having a night out. You and your wife and I'll bring Laura. You know, we're a couple now."

"That's good news, Barkow. Molly and I would love to get together."

"Fine. Discuss it with Molly and we'll set a date."

"Great. I'll get back to you on the Schmidt thing, okay?"

"You bet, see you later, Jim"

Barkow returned to their reserved table as Laura was on the last song of her set. He raised his glass to Terry for a refill. She nodded and went to the bar. Barkow noticed Adelita Ramos was just entering the nightclub. She was alone and took a table for two, set back from the dancefloor. When Terry brought his drink over, he said. "Terry, did you see Ms. Ramos come in?"

"Yes, she just took a table."

"Please ask her to join me and find out what she wants to drink."

"Right away, Boss." She hurried away.

Laura came to the table and sat down.

"Do you want anything to drink?" He asked.

"No, not now, Honey."

Barkow watched Adelita walking toward him and saw Terry, following her, pushing a chair. "Hi, Adelita, how's business?"

"Laura, you remember my Attorney, Adela Ramos."

"Of course," Laura said. "Good Evening, Adelita."

Terry brought the drinks and Barkow said, "My tab, Terry."

"I asked you over, Adela, to talk a few minutes of business, unless you're meeting someone."

"No, Barkow. I was working late with a client and just stopped by for a quick drink and to hear the lovely Laura sing."

"I'll be back on in about ten minutes." Laura said. "Do you have a favorite you'd like me to sing?"

"No, Laura. Anything you sing is perfect. You have a lovely voice."

"Thank you."

"What I had in mind, Adelita, was for you to draw up a partnership agreement between Laura Lee Logan and myself as equal partners in *Barkow's Blue Note*. I'll send over the details. She is to be a full and equal partner.

"Congratulations, Laura." Adelita said.

"Thank you, Adelita."

They chatted a bit until Laura returned to the piano. A while later Adelita left for home and Barkow spent the rest of the evening listening to the music with Laura singing every other song. Barkow was delighted when he noticed that most everyone seemed enraptured when Laura sang.

The weeks drifted by. Laura's penthouse apartment was under construction, the new hours for the nightclub were put into effect and business continued without a letup.

One day, Lieutenant Greenwell called and left a message for Barkow to meet him at the Police Station that evening at 7:00 p.m. Barkow arrived exactly at the time of the meeting.

"Hi, Jim, what's up?" He said when he saw the Lieutenant coming toward him."

"Hey, Barkow. Come on back to my office. You want a cup of coffee?

"Yeah. Black as usual."

"Here you go." He sat the cup on the desk as Barkow sat down.

"So, tell me how you got tangled up with Victor E. Schmidt?"

"He was calling the Blue Note and asking for me while I was in Belize. Wouldn't give his name or any contact number to my bartender, but called every once in a while. Then one day, after I came home, he called and Bobby set up a meet at seven that night. We met in my office and he said he wanted to hire me as a Government Agent for the CIA. He gave me a card saying he was a Director of CIA and laid out a dream package for me to go to work. When I pressed him for a phone number and contact address he balked at giving the info, so I threw him out"

"Well, I did some checking and found out, Victor actually is connected with the CIA. As soon as I started digging for information the person I was talking with clammed up and said he would have someone call me. I asked for his badge number and he hung up. Then I get a visit from the FBI office here in town and he wanted to know why I was checking into the CIA and where I got the name of Victor E. Schmidt."

"So, what did you tell him?" Barkow said.

"I told him it was a police matter and I would have to check a few things out before I could tell him anything. He's coming back tomorrow and I thought you may want to be there."

"Thanks, Jim. I appreciate it, and yes, I would like to sit in on the meeting."

"Apparently my calling stirred up a hornets nest," Jim said. They seemed awful touchy. The meet is set for 10:00 a.m. tomorrow."

"I'll be there." Barkow said. "Thanks again for the tipoff."

"No problem. See you tomorrow. I'm heading for home and some shuteye."

Barkow left the station and drove to the Blue Note. He spent the evening listening to Laura sing, talking with Bobby and Terry, and wondering about the strange happenings concerning the U.S. Government.

CHAPTER TWENTY-EIGHT

THE FBI AGENT arrived at the police station for the 10:00 a.m. meeting. He said his name was Dwight Henderson and brought with him an agent from CIA, who introduced himself as Herbert Spenser.

"It has come to our attention Greenwell that you have been inquiring about one of the officers in our department." The CIA agent spoke as if he was in charge of an interrogation.

Barkow immediately broke in and spoke bitterly. "The Lieutenant was merely asking if such an agent was actively a member of the CIA, on my behalf."

The man from Central Intelligence turned to Barkow. "Why would the Police be concerned about such matters?"

"Because I'm a citizen of Phoenix, Arizona and I asked him to. For Christ's sake, Spenser, it's not a major incident in the turning of this planet. It so happens I was visited by a person who claimed he was a Director of CIA in the United States and that he wanted to hire me as a covert agent. I asked Officer Greenwell if he could check and see if such a person did work for CIA."

"So why, Barkow, would you have even considered the word of a stranger?"

Barkow's eyes narrowed. "Because he gave me a business card that stated his name was Victor E. Schmidt and that he was a CIA Director of the United States. I believed him an imposter because he didn't act quite portentous enough. Oh, it's true, he was definitely pompous enough and displayed a snotty attitude of self-importance, but I wanted to check. One can't be too careful these days, don't you agree, Spenser?"

Spenser ignored Barkow and turned to the FBI agent, "Thank you for bringing this to my attention, Henderson. I'll handle it from here. Your cooperation is greatly appreciated."

Henderson stood up and said, "Good day Gentlemen." And walked out of the office.

"Henderson meant well but is sometimes a little portentous." Spenser said.

"In that case," said Lieutenant Greenwell. "I will excuse myself and you two may talk all day. I have work to do." With that said, he stood up, winked at Barkow and left the office.

"I do have some things to discuss with you, Barkow. I don't have an office in this city but...."

Barkow broke in on him and said, "I have one, Spenser, and it's private. If you follow me over, I'll talk as long as you have something to say."

"I cannot follow you as I came with the FBI."

"No problem, Spenser, you ride with me," Barkow said.

When they arrived and were settled in Barkow's office, Spenser spoke from his side of the desk.

"First of all, let me tell you about Victor. He is a rather odd sort to begin with. He is one of many directors, but not *the* Director. You see, for decades, he was an absolutely brilliant agent and was promoted to a director position. Then a bullet creased his skull near the temple and gouged a furrow that took away a portion of his mental capacity. He still works for the Government because of his many years of honorable service and is allowed to maintain his position as a courtesy. The Bureau uses him to do some cleanup on dead end cases and occasionally to check out new employees being considered for hiring. How he got your case in his mix of duties, I don't know, but I will take steps to see he does not bother you again. He is never to be involved in the hiring of agents."

"Why is your office interested in me?" Barkow said.

"The CIA is searching for a person to take a position quite similar to what Victor described to you. What we need, is to hire a man for The Central Intelligence Agency to work clandestinely as a special operative. One that can handle sensitive information which could jeopardize national security. The CIA is a very large, federal department and has operations all over the world in various sectors. This job requires an agent from, shall we say, a seamy background. Someone who is accustomed to taking matters into his own hands and if required can kill without remorse. That's why, although you do not meet the standard college requirements, you could still be hired."

"Seamy background, eh?" Barkow said. "How often would I be called and is there any average amount of time per each interval of employment?"

"You would be called upon whenever a man of your talent is required. Length of course varies with your expertise in completing the orders given you. Sometimes it is accomplished within twenty-four hours. Other times it can run up to a month or possibly more. Normally there would only be a need for your service perhaps once or twice a year. Understand, you are not being hired to go about killing people. It's more like being able to take command and get done what your orders require to be accomplished.

"Your investigative process and findings must be kept very private, due to the sensitivity regarding the nature of the work. We already know you would qualify, providing you have not engaged in unlawful practices since your discharge from the Armed Service. The Central Intelligence Agency has alliances all over the world, but you would be on your own. If you got into trouble, depending on what caused it, the Government could and perhaps would, disavow any knowledge of knowing you at all. There will be no record of your employment in the Federal Archives. That is the nature of the work, if you decide to accept the offer. You would be extremely well compensated in both monetary and tangible rewards. In fact you could practically write your own ticket."

"I need to consider this a while," Barkow said. "Whom do I contact with my terms, if I decide to accept?"

"You may call this number and ask for Spenser, Agent Herbert Spenser." He placed a business card on Barkow's desk.

"Is there any time limit on this offer?"

"It is open until the position has been filled."

"Will I be notified when this job has been filled?"

"No. You will have to call me when you decide to accept or reject the position."

Barkow stood up and held out his hand. "Until we speak again, Spenser," he said.

Spenser rose from his chair and grasped Barkow's hand. "Until then, cheerio," he said.

Barkow opened his office door for the agent and closed it behind him. He returned to his desk and removed the hidden recorder from a drawer, where it had documented the entire conversation between him and the CIA agent. He removed the small disc and after locking up, drove to his penthouse and stopped off at the lobby to speak with Hank at the front desk.

"Hello, Hank. How are things going?"

"Not bad. Not bad at all, and how are things with you and the lovely, Laura?"

They made small talk about various sports teams and then Barkow said. "I have a feeling, Hank, someone may be checking me out. Will you keep an eye out for any strangers who may be lurking about the building?"

"You bet, Barkow. I usually do, but will stay extra alert and let you know if anything turns up."

"Thanks, Hank. See you later."

He took the elevator up and entered the penthouse as usual, Laura came to meet him, with a hug and a kiss, as soon as he stepped inside.

"How did the meeting go?" she said as they went into the living room.

"About like I thought it would. Nothing of importance." He'd decided to let the idea marinate in his thoughts for a while, holding the viewpoint it required no discussion until some inner decision was made.

"I have some new tile samples for the bathroom and I want you to come take a look at them and give me your opinion." She gave him a wicked little smile that spoke volumes about their first shower together.

"Why do you need my opinion," he asked with a smile.

"I may want to seduce you in my bathtub some day and don't want you to dislike my tile. So it's important you approve now."

"Seduction works no matter what the tile looks like," he said, as hand in hand they went to her side of the penthouse, presently under construction.

The days passed into weeks which in turn became months. Laura's apartment was finished and furnished, although she continued to sleep with Barkow and spent most of her time in his rooms. All her clothes, including two hundred and eighteen pairs of shoes, were in a custom built closet that covered fifteen hundred square feet. There were racks of hanging dresses, gowns, suits, etc. Drawers of different sizes filled a four foot high section of wall space, thirty feet in length. The long polished top and the bank of drawers was elegantly finished like cherry-wood furniture and displayed various works of art, backlit by indirect lighting on the top of its four foot height.

A delightfully furnished section of space with a large viewing window that looked out over the downtown section of Phoenix. Also a game table with comfortable chairs, used by Barkow and Laura for playing cards, cribbage and chess.

A modern kitchen, stocked with everything required for making a banquet, if it ever became necessary. Laura, for a change of pace, from time to time prepared dinner for the two of them, from which they would later retire to her bedroom for passionate lovemaking between black, satin sheets.

Barkow hired a maid service to come in every Monday for housekeeping. They lived a life of luxury on the penthouse floor of the complex that was fast becoming a building of upper class condominiums. Quietly, without anyone in the structure being aware, Barkow had taken legal control of the entire building through the Law Office of Adelita Ramos.

—END—

ABOUT THE AUTHOR

Archie J. Hoagland was born in Nebraska City, Nebraska at the height of the Great Depression in 1932. He grew up in the farmlands of Nebraska, Oklahoma, Colorado, Utah, and Oregon. Because his father was a sharecropper, his family moved every year. Archie never attended the same school more than one year until he attended high school in Hillsboro, Oregon.

He dropped out as soon as his age allowed him to join the US Navy and served his three-year enlistment, plus one more for President Truman because the Korean War was raging. Assigned as an amphibious landing craft (LCVP) coxswain, he was involved in every amphibious operation in the Korean War, attached as ship's company aboard the USS *Cavalier APA-37*, an amphibious personal attack ship.

Archie is also a retired businessman, a member of the Benevolent and Protective Order of Elks (BPOE) for over forty years, a published poet, and a sculptor who works in terra cotta. He's the father of six sons and has seventeen grandchildren and four great grandchildren.

CPSIA information can be obtained at www.ICGtesting.com
Printed in the USA
BVOW08s2142240216

438003BV00002B/28/P